The Connection
Family First

T.S. Mcclain

Cadmus Publishing
www.cadmuspublishing.com

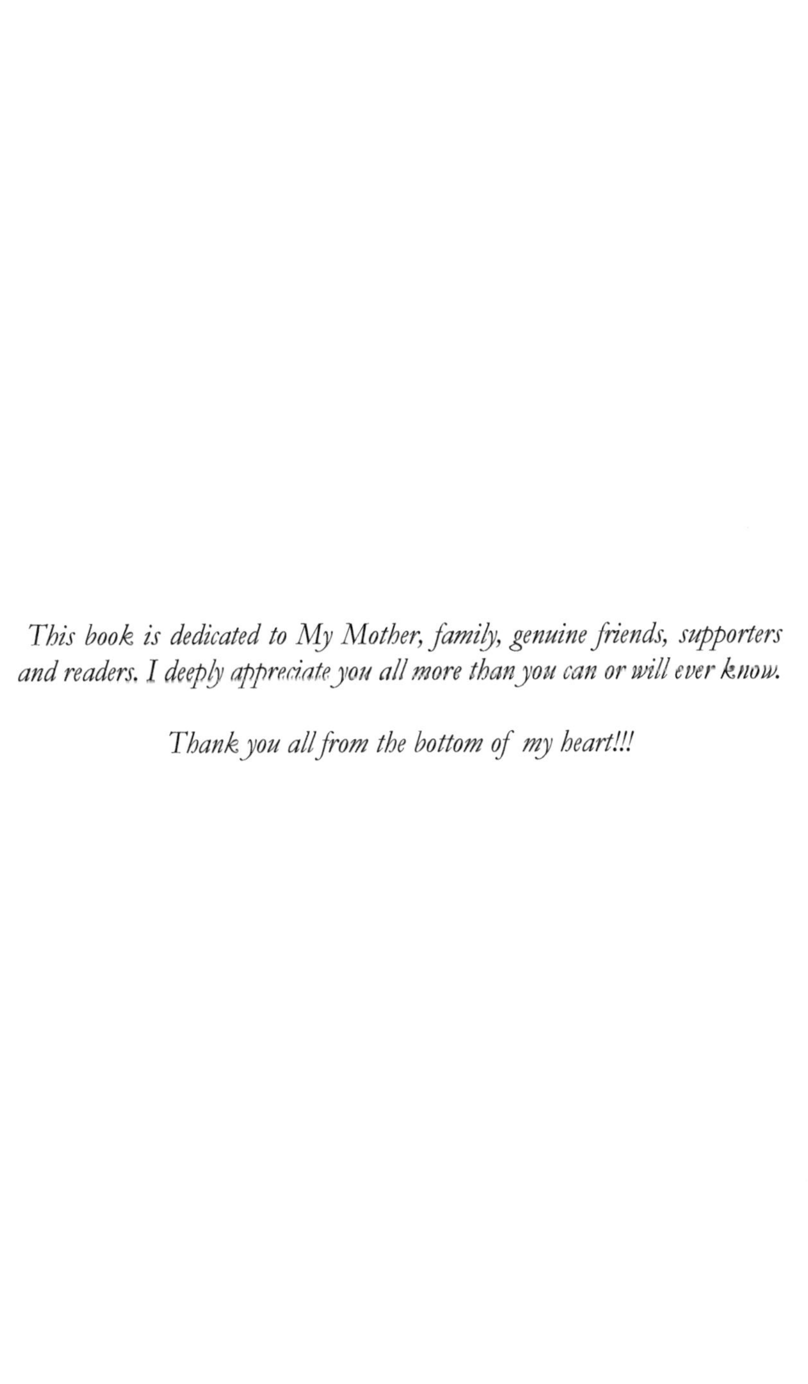

This book is dedicated to My Mother, family, genuine friends, supporters and readers. I deeply appreciate you all more than you can or will ever know.

Thank you all from the bottom of my heart!!!

Foreword

I was born to fight. Right now, at this exact minute, I stand fighting for my life serving a 65-year prison sentence, in a Connecticut prison, which leaves me with pure determination towards getting my freedoms back and out of the possession of this supposed to be free, but unjust legal system.

The process hasn't been anything nice, nor have it been easy, yet what it hasn't been is anything that I can't handle. My Islamic faith and unwavering belief in my creator, The Almighty Allah (God), helps me understand and know the height on the mountain I am able to climb.

To stand up and fight against any machine, single man or government is to be 100% sure not to lay down when faced with adversity. The grind is real.

What I want my readers to take from this is, always stand up and never give up on what you believe in. The blows you may have to take might knock you backwards for a moment, they may even knock you down, though when you manage to get back up you'll only be stronger having taken such mighty blows.

-T.S. Mcclain

Acknowledgements

Special thanks to:

First, to Allah, the almighty. Without him I do not know where my mental would be.

To my big momma, may you rest in peace. I wish the world could've gotten to know the person I knew. To my kids, Tajah Jr. Na'tajah, Taijon, Tsa'tajah, Keyiza and my grandsons, L.J., Na'jah and granddaughter, Taj'anna, I hope I spelled that right, as well as their mothers, I appreciate every one of y'all for letting me still play my part in their lives.

To my siblings, Tiger, Wink, and Weezziey, Little Sis. I love you a lot and I appreciate everything you do for me and everybody else.

To all my nephews and nieces, it's so many to name, but ya'll all know who you are, the same go for my real ones, such as Code-Red, my Big Cuz, Crazy Erica, Mable, Curty, G-Bell, D. Meyers and all the women, ya'll know exactly who you are that answers that phone, show up on those visits, etc. simply to put a smile on my face or get me to put one on yours, I appreciate all that's real.

And,

I won't forget, Tharesa, my second mother, I am still trying to write your character in one of these books. Aunt Linda, just like my Aunt Bert, rest in peace, you have shown me real love and my godmother Dennise, I love you all… Family first.

-T.S. Mcclain

"When a gangster becomes political is when white America starts to tremble."

-Malcolm-X

Table of Contents

Prologue 1
Loco 5
Rah-mere .17
Fernando .23
Pedro 27
Detective Banks 31
Fernando .36
Orlando 38
Detective Banks 40
Rah-Mere .43
Knuckles .46
Detective Banks 49
Orlando 52
Rah-mere .54
Knuckles .57
Fernando .62
Ayah 66
Detective Banks 69
Rah-mere .72
Rah-mere .75
Detective Banks 79
Rah-mere .82
Detective Banks 85
Fernando .87
Detective Banks 90
Loco 94
Loco 97

PROLOGUE

The year was nineteen eighty-eight, the time when nothing was making more dead presidents than the coke game. Cocaine, known for being the rich man's drug was being snorted, shot and sold by any lucky dealer that was able to get their hands on some. If you had a plug (connection), then you was known as the man to see, and who'd supplied all the big time Hollywood actors, ball players and whoever else looking to get their taste of the snow.

Only nineteen and dying for his shot at being Connecticut's newest kingpin, Loco dreamed of being the go-to man on the East Coast. He believed he had his own connect, the time in on the streets and was well known for leaving a trail of dead bodies behind him if anyone tested his authority. Waiting any longer to take his spot and seat on the throne was far from his thoughts. Now was his time. And it was gonna be all his, is what Loco was thinking, though there was one more thing he knew he had to do.

Pulling the black on black Cadillac El Dorado he was wheeling through the East side of Bridgeport's streets, pulling over at an East Main Street curb, his pager in hand Loco swaggered over to the sidewalk pay phone.

"Yo, meet me at the mansion," was the only words he said to the person on the other end of the phone.

Back behind the wheels of his ride and now anxiously clutching his .44 revolver, Loco was ready to fulfill his dreams.

Haviera, the East Coast kingpin, someone who'd found and gave an eleven-year-old homeless and abandoned Loco a shot, as well as a safe place on his team, stood confident holding onto his dignity refusing to beg for his life, as Loco pointed his revolver at him, and threatened he would blow his head off.

"How do you think you're gonna get out of here if you pull that trigger? You know you will never make it out of here alive, so kid, why don't you put that damn thing down and let's forget this ever happened," Haviera said, smirking a smile of deceit.

"Well, I would agree with you if that was a worry of mine, but it's not. I think you need to ask yourself how did I ever get past your security in the first place," smiling Loco said gesturing at Haviera's main bodyguard, being held at gunpoint by one of his soldiers.

Haviera, shaking his head at what he was now clearly thinking, for the first time he was questioning his people. He had always made sure to take good care of every one of them, from the top soldiers down to the gardeners. He was starting to worry, though he would never allow Loco to notice.

"Bring him over here," Loco ordered, cocking his automatic, while his soldier pushed the guard forward.

Standing inches away from his boss, the man he had protected for more than thirty years, looking Haviera in his eyes as one cold tear fell from his, the bodyguard reached into his waistline, pulling out his Glock .45. Pulling the trigger two times, he sent Haviera backwards, with his eyes still open and no brains left in his head. Smiling, he turned acknowledging the soldier who'd held his gun on him and then to Loco. Giving Loco a big hug and kiss on both cheeks, he thanked and praised his new boss and kingpin of the coast.

✦ 3 ✦

"Man can be his worse enemy, especially when he don't pay attention to the hands that he shakes. Make sure they match the smiles, and you'll learn who's the fakes."

-T.S. Mcclain

LOCO

I have been waiting for this day for a long time, and now that it's here I am feeling real good about myself. All I gotta do now is get in and out of New York City with the three hundred bricks (kilos) that's waiting for me without any problems, and I'll be able to begin my new life as the go-to supplier on the East Coast.

Leaving Bridgeport, traveling south on I-95 I made sure to keep my third eye on my rearview mirror, checking for any suspicious-looking vehicles and faces that might be tailing me.

With only twenty minutes away until crossing the city's line I turned my music up allowing it to blast, and my soul to become one with my favorite rappers, Eric B. and Rakim's newest hit "Paid in Full", never noticing the silver with tinted windows Jeep shadowing my every maneuver since entering the interstate, staying a couple blocks' length away the whole way.

New York City and its everyday and all night hustle and bustle I have always loved.

Today it's hot as hell out here, and every one of these Big Apple streets is crowded more than they normally are, looking like the devil his self has brought his heat down on every one of the high rises that held a body, forcing them all outside.

The traffic was bumper to bumper and filled with road raging limousine and yellow cab drivers, racing to their next stop light.

Driving through the Harlem streets taking Amsterdam not wanting to ride on hot ass Broadway, I made a left at 142nd where I quickly found an open parking spot that would allow me to hide my Connecticut plates.

Stepping out into the double-parked cars and children playing skipball streets, I felt as if I was back home on a Bridgeport block, I was comfortable.

Walking up three blocks to 145th I had no feeling that I was being watched, only the feeling of excitement seeing the connect's drop car, a custom body built money green Beamer sitting on the latest rims and tires, waiting at the curb for me.

I didn't want to look obvious, so I walked directly into McDonald's instead of to the still running and loaded luxury car, to order a quick meal to go.

Checking my iced out Presidential Rolex, I knew I had spent enough time inside the restaurant that would make it look like I had parked the car and only ran in for a quick second. With my orange soda and bagged meal in hand, I stepped out onto the crowded Broadway sidewalk, heading straight for my new fortune.

The bricks was perfectly packed in four custom compartments, where I could easily get to them with one push on the AC button and a double pull on the emergency brake at the same time, but only when the transmission was in park.

Pulling away from the Washington Heights curb, heading straight for the Cross Bronx Expressway and the I-95 North highway, I was feeling more confident than ever of my new place at the throne. What the plug (connect) failed to let me know about, was the deal he'd made a month earlier with one of New York City's dirtiest 21 Jump Street Boys, after being indicted on a chop shop ring where him and forty other members of his crew had been named and caught in a raid of his shop. Arrested and charged with ten kilos of pure heroin found in one of his shop walls, he was set free after agreeing to give up one of his biggest buyers, specifically one from out of state.

Traveling with a definite life sentence was starting to fuck with my nerves. This shit never happened to me before when riding dirty, I'm talking continuous flutters, that feeling you get when you're over-anxious, and the same one that makes you think you're about to shit on yourself.

"Ahhhh, fuck! I am not pulling over," I yelled out to no one, gripping the steering wheel. "Why the fuck is this happening?"

When approaching the Jerome and Westchester Avenues' traffic, I could see that making it through was not going to be a quick process. The closer I got the faster the vehicles in front of me seemed to be piling up, making getting through even more difficult.

I had always been able to calm my anxiousness with focusing on something else, so I reminisced back to my vacation to Miami, and the one night stand I had two months earlier.

Dressed wearing a peach-color linen V-neck, the same color trousers being held up by a five-hundred-dollar Gucci belt, a pair of Gucci loafers, my rose gold diamond-encrusted chain hanging from my neck, my wrist looking like it was dipped in ice, goatee perfectly trimmed and my dreads hanging across my shoulders and down my back making my rail-thin 6'2" frame look longer than it really was, I walked into a South Beach Gucci store looking to purchase a pair of shades, to go along with what I was wearing.

Entering the busy store immediately my breath was taken, seeing this sexy Dominican chick standing behind the store's counter and operating the register. She didn't see me but I saw her, and I knew I had to have her.

When meeting a person, man or woman, I always make it my business to place my confidence on display at the first appearance of me, especially women I like. Making my way I confidently strutted up to the counter causing the possible Ms. Dominicana to step back, and away from the register.

"Excuse me, can I help you?" the curly jet-black hair, honey-color skin and curvy body woman reacted.

"Margaret. Margaret is your name, right?" I asked, reading the nametag she had pinned to the uniform she had on. "My name is Loco, and I would like to get to know you."

Looking into Margaret's almond-shaped brown eyes I could tell she was thinking something, and it wasn't wanting me to get the fuck away from her. Her long stare and noticeable perky nipples was assuring me that my presence had caused between her curvaceous thighs to react, just as I expected. I could tell she wanted me as bad as I wanted her but wasn't gonna show it yet.

Flashing her pretty smile, dimples in both cheeks and pearly white teeth she said, speaking in Spanish, "How can I help you, sir?" Acting as if she never heard a word I said.

"Yes you can. You can start by dropping the customer service stuff. I am sure you heard what I said. I would like to take you out tonight, and you should just say yes."

"Excuse me? Who do you think you are? I guess I'm supposed to just say yes to a complete stranger, and end up in your refrigerator at the end of the night, huh? I don't know you, and I can see you're not from anywhere around here due to that funny-sounding accent you got."

"No, I'm not from down here or the South, I'm from up North, Bridgeport, Connecticut. I know plenty that would agree with me, that it is your country-sounding accent that sounds funny. But all jokes aside, I came down here for some fun, before I start a new job. Now, your feisty ass should stop giving me such a hard time and come help me enjoy myself. What do you say?"

"You must not speak Spanish," recognizing I had responded in English, Margaret said.

"I don't. I mean I do understand, and can a little bit but rather not, and use my English. My mother was black and my father he's Cuban. These are all the things you can get to know about me if you just say yes, and let me take you out."

"We will see."

"So I guess that's a yes."

"No, it's not. I got customers to take care of, so please step aside, Mr. Up North. If you're still around when I'm done, then we will see." Margaret flashed that soft smile of hers at me, after greeting a tired of waiting in line teenager.

All of my life because of my Latin features, though I look more African-American than anything, people would ask if I spoke Spanish. They would go out of their way speaking the language, not knowing that I don't fully understand what they were saying.

Growing up on the East Side it was always known as Baby Puerto Rico, being how there're Puerto Ricans on every block and at every corner you turn. All through the streets you'd noticed the low riders and sexy island girls, smell the forbidden pork in the air and hear the Spanish chatter.

I never grasped the full language, yet enough that I knew would protect my neck. The East Side was a shiesty place, and you better had at least knew some of what was always going down.

My attention was solely on the Gucci shades I have finally decided to purchase, when Margaret's beautiful ass interrupted.

"Those cost eight-fifty," she said, in the deepest country accent I had ever heard. "Are you looking for something cheaper? You should look over on that wall," she pointed over at another wall filled with shades at the back of the store.

"Oh, you think I can't pay for these."

"Look, my job is only to help, not tell you what you can or can't afford. I guess you don't need my help, so when you need me I'll be over there."

Margaret walked away from me knowing I would be captivated by her 5'6" and curvaceous body frame, hair hanging down to her plumped ass and walk that said my pussy is the one. She was right, and now I wanted her even more. I was ready to make a boss player statement, something I knew would make Margaret understand how I was living, so I walked up to her register where she was back at making it known that money wasn't a thing. "I want every pair on that wall," I said, pointing at the most expensive shades in the store.

"Excuse me? Those start at the eight-fifty price I said, and up."

"That won't be a problem, I want all of them."

All thirty pair of shades bagged, I figured I make my last push at getting the dollar signs now in her eyes, Margaret, to go out with me.

"What do you think now? What time should I be picking you up?" I smirked.

"Here's my address, and do not be late," Margaret pushed a folded register size piece of paper into my shirt pocket. Her pussy now super wet needing a change of her thong.

Making it to pick Margaret up earlier than our agreed upon time, I was sure her pussy was gonna taste just as good as she came to the door looking. Her dress and shoes wasn't anything expensive to talk about, but she was rocking whatever unnamed brand swag like that shit came off a Paris runway. She was looking smashing and I was ready to play the how long is it gonna take for me to get Margaret's clothes off her game. I didn't know nothing about or where to go on South Beach so I allowed her to lead.

We spent the whole night enjoying all the finest food, expensive champagne and entertainment money could buy before drunkenly ending the night at my rented facing the beach five-star hotel room.

From the time we entered the three master bedroom size room, we couldn't keep our hands off each other. Spending all of what was left of the morning sucking and fucking on one another, we did until we both had passed out, and being awakened by the rising Florida sun.

My night with Margaret was fun and fucking her was just how I figure it would be, but not knowing I was being watched and followed really fucked with my head. When I woke up Margaret was no longer laying beside me, causing me to quickly get myself up and out of the bed in search of my wallet. Bare ass naked as I was brought into this world I ran across the huge room where I found not one thing was missing, yet the hotel's phone was now ringing.

"Hello."

"Hey, I'm sorry for how I left, but I do have a job, remember. I called to at least to let you know I did have a great time with you and also to tell you, I was approached this morning here at the store by some weird-looking guy with a similar funny-sounding up North accent as yours. He did say he was from out of state and that he was looking for my new lover from Connecticut," Margaret said.

Who was this person, I did not know, but one thing was clear, whoever it was he had to have been following me. What was not clear was since when.

I was almost home free passing the South Norwalk Exit Fifteen, "Only twelve more to go until, and I will be back on comfortable grounds," is what I was thinking.

The fluttering in my stomach was no longer, but still I wasn't feeling like my normal self. My nerves were still not calm. Still trying to get my complete hold on them I thought about Jane, my pregnant girlfriend waiting at home for me to walk through the door.

Unable to contact Margaret I had been treating Jane real fucked up, not spending any time like I use to with her. I couldn't keep Margaret and the fun we had down in Miami off my mind. Jane was six months pregnant, the same amount of time since I last saw Margaret, which weighed heavily on my mind. When she asked for a simple used car, feeling guilty I took her car shopping, buying her the car of her dreams, a brand new fully-loaded pink with snow white interior BMW.

"What the fuck is this?" Snapping back to reality I said, not able to believe what I was looking at. The same silver with tinted windows Jeep I'd saw when passing through the toll-booths. Now it was in my rearview mirror, directly behind me with its flashing lights on wanting me to pull over to the shoulder of the highway. "How the fuck could this be happening right now? I'm only minutes away from the fucking stash house. Should I go all out and shoot it out with whoever this is or should I trust that the custom compartments will do just what they suppose to," I spoke to myself. Quickly stashing my .9 I decided pulling over expecting everything to go smooth.

Four Months Later...

The plug it seemed had fallen off the face of the earth, running away to one of those South American jungles where they grew and made the cocaine he had been smuggling into the country, knowing when the Twelve (police) had pulled me over and went directly to the stash boxes, I would then know it was him who gave me up to them. With the bricks, all three hundred kilos, in his possession, Detective Banks was now asking that I meet him to talk about us doing business.

The only business I was interested in was getting my coke back and out of his crooked hands, and nothing else, though he had different plans.

"This would be his last time robbing anybody," I said promising myself.

The second I stepped out of the Beamer to take a seat in his back seat as he asked, I knew things wasn't going how I thought they would. Although I was able to stash the gun, which left me with no worries about anything being found that would cause me to be arrested, still I was kicking myself in the ass for not choosing to shoot it out.

The way the detective was so confident about letting me keep my freedom over going to jail for possibly the rest of my life, told me his crooked ass had robbed other dealers before. He was a straight up Jackboy.

I didn't want Detective Banks to see what I was driving, so I parked at the side of the diner where he asked me to meet him. I did not like meeting where it would be covered by Bridgeport cops in seconds, if I decided to just take the pig out, but my whole life fortune is what was in question, so after parking my smoked-out gray color Z-28 out of view, I walked into White's Diner with getting my shit back only on my mind.

Stepping out of the chilly November weather into the not so busy diner, removing the cone head Champion hoody brought unwanted eyes that now made me their attention reminded me why I didn't want to meet there. For whatever reason the small crowd of customers looked uncomfortable seeing me walking in.

Surveying the not so big diner, I noticed and couldn't believe the balls on the red blotched skin complexion, no facial hair and looking like the average alcoholic standing up at the back of the place, Detective Banks, waving me over. Seeing the big ass smile on Bank's face, looking like he was so happy to see me took every bit of strength I had in me not to pull my heat out and empty the whole clip in his face, like I should've done the day four months ago when he first forced his self into my life. Now he's doing it again, though he has the upper hand, and I have to hear him out.

"I'm glad you came. I ordered you one," pushing a pre-ordered glass of tea at me Detective Banks greeted me, flashing his dingy brownish-yellow nicotine-stained teeth, putting a devilish grin on full display.

"I don't shake hands with pigs and fuck that tea, I'm only here to talk about one thing, and that's my coke, nothing else," I said refusing to shake hands.

"I see you're too good to have a glass of good tea with me."

"Look, I did not come here to play no games with you. Like I said, what's up with my bricks?"

Staring into Bank's cold blue eyes I could actually see his sinister thoughts building by the minute. The smirk he now was wearing on his face told me something wasn't right, yet I didn't know what that something was. The only thing I knew was how ready I was to smoke the shiesty motherfucker and leave him right where he was. "Can I take your order?" A vibrant-looking young black waitress approached the table, speaking to me who'd finally taken my seat.

"No, thank y…"

Detective Banks butted in. "You can get me another tea, but hot this time." Sending the tight body caramel complexion female away. "Now listen and listen closely. What I called you here for is greater to you than you getting those kilos back I took. And it comes with a one-way ticket that can spell death for some very important members of your family, if you don't do just as I order you to."

"Death! Order! My family! Motherfucker!" I went to pull my Glock from my waistline.

"Go right ahead, gangster. You kill me, my peoples will kill every and anything that holds worth to you, so you sit right there and let me show you how much I know about your life that you don't."

At that time all I could do was sweat, armpits, palms and nuts, wanting to reach over the not so wide table and send Banks to his maker, but I was beginning to understand that I couldn't, I had to listen to his bullshit. "Jane, you know her right, Loco? We would hate to see her pretty little face on the 6 o'clock news found dead because of your stupid decisions." He now had my complete attention.

Me and Jane had met in high school and had been together since. Her 5'3" stature, feisty attitude, perfectly proportioned with curvy thick thighs, a set of mango-size tits with nipples that you could always tell was hard, and beautiful shiny-looking silky skin, that looked like it could be mistaken for a piece of chocolate, was all that intrigued my curiosity, she had to be mine. Jane was a clear dime piece and the baddest bitch in the school. When everybody saw us, even the teachers, they just watched like they was witnessing two stars in their presence. We was the shit and the toilet paper it went in. Now this pig was sitting in front of me threatening to take her from me. I placed my hand under the front of my hoodie, now contemplating Detective Banks' death.

"And she's pregnant, with your future son," he said, causing me to shift in my seat.

"Now, please? Don't you let that bother you. Let me give you something else you need to know. That sexy little Dominican thing you have popped up and left down in Miami, Margaret, that is her name, right. Well, she's pregnant as well, and her doctor tells me she's having herself a little boy too."

"Is this pig serious? How the fuck do he know all of this," was what I was thinking. I wanted to destroy the piece of shit right then, but all I could think of was what if I did and even was he telling the truth that Margaret was really pregnant.

Detective Banks honestly had my head all fucked up. I could do nothing but sit across from him stuck, building in anger.

"What the fuck are you saying?" I snapped, causing the elderly couple sitting three booths away to turn in their seats to look back at us.

What I'd agreed to meet Banks for was no longer on my mind, only Jane, Margaret, our unborn kids and what the devil was going to say next.

"I have thoroughly done my homework on your life as you can see, and now I want my reward."

"Reward? Son of a bitch, you already got me for three hundred kilos. How much more of a reward are you looking for?"

"I want you gone in seventy-two hours. Out of this country and not to ever look back, not for anything at all. Do you get me? Do you hear what I'm saying to you?" Detective Banks blurted out, stunning me.

I had to give myself a long moment to let Detective Banks' words penetrate my brain.

I could not believe what I was hearing. I was sitting in front of Lucifer in the flesh. First he rob me for a fortune and now to protect it he's sitting here now threatening to kill my family if I don't exile from the country, leaving them behind.

"What if I chose not to?" The hot feeling in my blood forced me to ask.

"Then my people will take care of Margaret and Jane. You do know what I mean when I say take care, don't you?" Banks coldly answered.

The smirk he showed on his face ate straight through my heart, and he knew it.

"And Jane, I know how much you love her. I've ordered something specific and special for her. She will be decapitated and your son inside her will be cut out and chopped into small pieces, to be delivered to you. I can understand that murderous look in your eyes, I swear I do. I also understand that you can pull that piece you've been itching to pull out and use on me, believe me I do. Let me help you with this small bit of information. You can kill me if you like, because right now I am prepared to die, but those killers standing outside of Margaret and Jane's homes, they're waiting to hear or not hear from me. You kill me you kill both of them, so the decision you make now holds over their heads. Your best bet is to do as I am telling you to. You now have seventy-one hours left being you have already wasted one sitting here with me exercising your hardest gangster looks."

I could not take any more of Satan's bullshit, so I got up pushing my way up and out of the tight booth.

Standing over and looking down into Detective Banks' ice-cold eyes, I blasted his face with the thickest coated piece of hog-spit before walking away, knowing I was going to have to do just as he ordered me to, or sign my own unborn sons' death certificates.

RAH-MERE

Twenty-two years later...

I had been hearing a lot about these Dominicans who just showed up, not only in Bridgeport but all over Connecticut, and they was moving big time weight, coke and heroin. One name that keeps coming up is the nigga's, I seen in the club the other night when me and my crew was out fishing for our next victim. I was told he was down here from Florida and he's connected to some real big people whose money can get a nigga touched no matter where he is at, or who he's down with. All that information I got about him, only made me want that motherfucker even more. I wanted to snatch his pretty ass right then and there but Knuckles talked me off of it. This is my city, my state, and if anybody gonna be sucking the paper out of this bitch it's gonna be The Get Down or Lay Down Boyz. And as long as I got this breath in me, and I can squeeze my trigger I'm gonna bust my gun making sure, whoever gotta put me in the dirt for it.

"This motherfucker is about to feel us. When we're done his peoples will know to take their business back to the South and leave ours alone," was what I was thinking, while me and my team was laying in the bushes seeing our target walking towards us and approaching his Range Rover carrying two Louis Vuitton suitcases.

"Put your hands up, motherfucker!" Me and the team, all six of us, wearing masks and gloves jumped out of the dark, a perfect blind spot in the parking lot, with our guns pointed at Tito, the front man of the Florida connection, catching him off guard and before he could reach for his pistol or stick his key into the Rover's door.

Placing the suitcases down and his hands over his head Tito started to plead, throwing around promises for exchange for his life until J.O. had introduced the butt of his pump to his jaw, dropping him to his knees and filling his mouth with blood.

Tito showed up in Connecticut with the plan that he would set up shop there. Connecticut was nothing like Florida, and surely nothing like Miami, South Beach, where Tito was from, though it was a perfect spot he and his partner liked and was determined to add to their operation, supplying and flooding with all kinds of drugs. Bridgeport, Hartford, and New Haven was the most dangerous in the state with Bridgeport being the biggest city of the three, so that was where he chose to run his business from, yet Tito nor his partner ever gave who ran it a care. All they cared about was how they was gonna take over the coke and dope game. Staring now down the barrels belonging to The Get Down or Lay Down Boyz, Tito wished they had.

I am twenty-three years old, and have been out here holding my city down for as long as I can remember. If anybody think I'm gonna sit back and not drop a body when somebody that's not from the bridge (Bridgeport) comes trying to move in, or take over, they're out of their fucking mind. I don't give a fuck about who they are or where they came from, you can put your life on it, they're gonna kiss the fucking ground.

I have been watching my mother suffer, losing weight waiting for a man to return to her, for years, so my heart is frozen cold for men. I don't wait for nothing, I go and take it.

Jane, Rah-mere's mother, was only six months pregnant with Rah-mere when his father up and left her, without saying a word.

The lovesick Jane fell into a years-long depression that caused serious anxiety and her to experience several breakdowns. She was not able to work, or take care of her only son. As soon as Rah-mere was able to take care of his self, he was forced to do nothing but take care of her. Her once perfectly proportioned body was now a blown-out frame, and the shiny chocolate skin complexion she always had that made her one of the finest chicks Bridgeport had ever seen, was now a dry ashy-looking dark brown color, leaving her far from the dime piece she was.

I had a front row seat witnessing my mother's condition get worse until it eventually killed her, taking her away from me and leaving me, a fourteen-year-old boy, on my own. That shit ripped my little heart right out of my chest. What was I gonna do? The only answer was to hit the streets and make somebody feel my pain, so that was just what I did, me and a couple of friends I knew understood my pain, getting ours the ski-mask way.

Knuckles, him and me, we came up living right next door to each other. His pops was gone, mother was in the streets fucked up on that crack, leaving him to raise his self just like I was. Both of us was kids, and understood one another completely. Coming up my soap, cereal, sandwich, no matter what it was was his. All we had was us. Pain, Lefty, Gunem, and J.O., four cats whose names was ringing in the city for not giving a fuck about catching a 187 (murder), me and Knuckles knew we had to link with. I always did know and was cool with the craziest one of their crew Wax, so us connecting was simple as a conversation.

Standing rail thin and 6 feet I towered over the short dark skin complexion Tito, mask still on though he could see my chip-tooth and menacing grin. Placing my Beretta to his bloody jaw I said, making sure he heard me, "All we want is the money and drugs. If you wanna get out of this alive you'll do exactly as I say and give us what we came for. You try and play hero, and he'll show you that this ain't no movie script." I pointed over towards J.O., who was ready to strike again. "We have been watching you for weeks, so don't play me. I want that duffle you brought here the other day, as well as those suitcases you stashed over at your condo yesterday."

I could see the cinnamon color leaving Tito's complexion, hearing me tell him about his every move he'd made when believing nobody was around. He was losing oxygen, and his complexion was a reddish pale color brown now. Hanging his head, resting his chin on the soaked bloody shirt, I could tell he was ready to give us whatever we wanted. This look I had seen on so many other occasions. That look a nigga get in his eyes, when he recognize that he has no chance at winning. You can catch the hardest motherfucker, I don't care if he done caught a hundred bodies, he's gonna have that same defeated look in his eyes.

"Don't worry, you can have it all, just don't kill me! I'm gonna give all of it to you." Still holding his broken jaw Tito got out, trying to save his life.

After the area around Tito's mother's mini mansion was thoroughly checked and cleared by Pain, J.O. with his pump still pressing against a pleading Tito's back, myself and the rest of the team rushed him into his mother's basement.

"Let's move! We do not got all day," Knuckles said, barking at Tito, same time pointing his shotty at his head as he pulled two large oversize duffle bags from a fake-looking wall, meant to look as if it was cement and unmoveable.

"Who the fuck is that?" I was thinking, listening, hearing a squeak coming from the floor above us, and seeing them gripping their weapons, Pain, Wax, and Lefty, moving in unison over to the stairs. All three with their guns drawn and ready, prepared to snatch the soul out of whoever decided to open the basement's door.

Dropping his head in prayer for his elderly mother's life, was all Tito could do.

"Come on, let's get up out of here, we got one more place to go," leading the team out of the dimly lit basement, I said.

"Move it, hurry up!" Wax shoved Tito in the middle of his back forward with his sawed-off. He was thirsty to taste blood and hoping that Tito flinched so he could have a reason to put one in the back of his head.

"I love this shit," carrying one of the filled with stacks of bills bags, inside eight hundred thousand wrapped in rubber bands and all hundred dollar bills, Gunem with one, Knuckles with the other, speaking said, on they way out of the house.

Getting in Tito's condo with guns in hand and a bloody Tito at gunpoint, I knew was gonna be a challenge, but it had to be done.

Instead of the whole crew going in as we did over at the first spot, somebody was gonna have to stay with the money, and that person had to only be who I trusted the most, Knuckles. The only one I know I can trust with my life. So Knuckles stayed with the bags while Lefty, the best driver of us all keep the Escalade running and ready in case we needed a fast got away from the scene. Using the condo's side entrance, which played as a blind spot allowed me, Gunem, Wax and J.O., each at one side of Tito with him in the middle, to move through the well-lit building. Making it to Tito's condo door we was in and out quickly, leaving with two more Louis Vuitton suitcases, the very same ones I knew he had stashed there days earlier, inside fifty thousand and forty perfectly packaged kilos, twenty in each one. Before leaving I made sure that Tito was tied down to his bed frame and unable to free himself, though when myself, J.O. and Gunem had made it back to the Escalade where Lefty and a anxious ready-to-go Knuckles waited was when I noticed Wax hadn't left Tito's with us. I could only imagine what he was up to.

The whole time we had Tito under our control, Wax had been mumbling some shit about what he wanted to do to him that I could not ever make out. He was still upstairs with Tito, and I do not even want to think about what that wicked motherfucker was up there doing. "I just hope he bring his ass on so we can get up out of this bitch," was the only thing I was thinking.

Wax had waited some time to get Tito alone, so that he could get his own shit off. The rest of the team was satisfied with the drugs and money they'd gotten Tito for, not Wax, he wanted blood. Like a junkie needing his fix with Tito tied down and laying flat out on his back, in the center of his king size bed, he jumped on top of him straddling Tito biting off both his ears, lips and nose. Drenched enjoy the taste of blood and feasting on Tito's flesh, before leaving Wax ended all of his victim's pain for good squeezing four bullets into the center of his chest, using his equipped with a silencer .40 Glock.

Rushing to the Escalade he wondered why everyone was staring at the trophy he had hanging from his bloody mouth. The first to speak with a look on his face that showed he was disgusted Knuckles asked, "What the fuck did you do?"

Swallowing what was left of Tito's ears, with a big smile on his face and blood still dripping down his chin onto his shirt, Wax answered causing all members to shake their heads in disbelief, "Shit, I have been hungry all day, I had to eat something," he answered.

FERNANDO

The last time me and Tito spoke he told me he was on his way over to his mother's spot, the place where we both felt was a perfect spot to stash the money being who would suspect his elderly and frail mother would be sitting on such a load of cash, to get ready to meet the accountant, Gomez. I've spoken to Gomez several times over the last few hours, he's telling me Tito has never contacted him once. I hate to allow these fucked up thoughts to cross my mind, but money can find a way to be the cause of a person's dishonor, especially a couple millions of it.

Me and Tito have been like brothers, inseparable since the first time we met, he was 10 and me eleven and a half. Hell fucking no he wouldn't run off with a measly one-point-six in cash. Something was up and I had to get down to the bottom of what it was. "I swear, if Gomez has anything to do with this, his ass will become food for my babies," I told myself.

"Gomez, have you heard from him yet?" I spoke gripping my cellphone extra tight and holding it to my ear, hoping the accountant would have new information that Tito did finally contact him.

"No boss, I haven't," Gomez answered in broken English.

"Okay, I want you to come back to Miami, so hop on the next flight. I need you to come keep my babies company."

"Your babies, boss, are you talking about the gators?"

"Yes, you fucking money-counting idiot! The fucking gators," I said raising my voice into the phone.

"I got you, boss, I'm sorry for questioning you. I will be sure that I get the next flight down there."

The fear in Gomez's voice was apparently hearable, and rightfully so. Who the fuck he thought he was questioning anyways?

My rise to Underboss status, twenty-three years old and the big dawg in Florida, specifically the cocaine capital, Miami, haven't been an easy one.

I was raised up in the shit, being introduced to the game by my stepfather, Choco, who was a well-known Cuban kingpin. Choco was loved by everybody in Miami. He was the man, a real big dawg and also the most dangerous motherfucker you could ever know, for one day you could literally find him and his peoples, some real vicious motherfuckers, out on the streets handing out food to anybody that stuck their hand out and took it, and the next he could send them same goons out to kill a whole family, babies and all.

My mother Margaret was introduced to Choco by her closest friend Norma, Tito's mother, when she had been six months pregnant with me. What I've heard is that her love for the Cuban Miami kingpin was on sight.

Wearing a fedora and dressed as sharp as a tack, Choco wore an expensive plum-hue color tailored suit topped with diamond cufflinks and sporting a huge rock on his pinky finger, along with his confidence that sucked the air out of the room making my mother's pussy throb, just as it did some years earlier, when my sperm donor had walked into her job at the high-end Gucci designer glasses store.

Taking care of and raising me Choco did that as if I was his very own, even after when my mother was found raped and robbed for the twenty kilos she'd been delivering for him. Found half-eaten outside a alligator swamp, Choco was sure to find who and what that ever touched her.

Stepping down from the top handing me the reigns to his empire, he made me the new and youngest Florida Boss. And I made sure that Tito was my right-hand man.

When Gomez was on the phone I could tell that he was confused and did not understand why I wanted him to come quick and keep my gators company. So I know the whole flight here his curiosity had to be killing him, trying to figure me out.

Watching the security cameras I can see that he did make it here, now being frisked and handing over his weapon to one of my burly-looking bodyguards, who took it and placed it at his waist. Walking through the massive corridors I could visually see how nervous that nigga was. When he walked into the room where I was, I made sure that he found me, standing outside of and throwing human body parts into my man-made swamp, feeding the very same two gators that was responsible for killing my mother.

I received them as a gift from Choco, who had them caught and brought to him where they became his pets, and now are mine. Every time I feed them I get a satisfaction that makes me feel like I am feeding my mother's soul as well.

Never turning around to greet the visibly shaking in his Air Force Ones Gomez I said over my shoulder, "I called you here because I blame you for Tito's sudden disappearing act," causing a choking sound to come abruptly bursting out of his mouth.

"Oh, no boss! Oh no! Not me! Not me boss!" was all Gomez could get out through his sudden loss of breath.

"Yes, you, you money-hungry motherfucker! And you're gonna pay for it."

"Pay for it! I had nothing, I have nothing to do with this," Gomez stammered on.

"He was supposed to meet you, and now you think I am supposed to believe you never did get to put your grubby fucking hands on my money. Here motherfucker, take this!"

I pulled my fo-fif (.45) from my lower back silencing Gomez forever, hitting him square between the eyes.

"Now, feed this piece of shit to the gators," I waved the bodyguard over. "And make sure that mess gets cleaned up," I said speaking of the massive amount of blood spreading across my red wooden floor.

I thought when I killed Gomez I would feel better about Tito's no-show, but I see now I am only feeling the opposite. Tito had to be found and I had the perfect two soldiers that'll do whatever it takes to find him for me. I picked up the phone.

PEDRO

When the boss called saying he needed us, me and Poncho, my twin brother, we both knew we had to get over to his compound quickly. Because of him is the only reason why Poncho had ever made it here to America, so whatever it was he needed from us we were ready to make happen.

Myself and Poncho, we was born in Mexico, and are identical twins, only I was born with this noticeable birthmark at the center of my forehead, though our 5'4" heights, tan complexions, petite builds and wavy auburn brownish hair color is all the same.

The day I was forced to leave Poncho behind after he'd broken his leg getting away from border patrol police was the worst day of my life. I went on making it across the border, he was caught and sent back to Mexico to live poor and like an animal, as we was that prompted us to leave. Running towards a better life was a shared dream of ours, so when I tried staying behind to help him, Poncho refused to allow it. Laying in pain and with a twisted the other way limb he begged that I continue on without him.

Making it to San Diego I hoped a bus ride to Florida, landing in Miami, right where Poncho and I had always wished we could go, there was where I made my name, bodying anything that had a price on his or her head. Murder was my business which made me the number one person to call, when the right people needed my services.

Introduced to Fernando, I was after reaching and touching a so-called untouchable man that Tito had hired me to make sure ended up in the dirt, turned out to be a day I will never forget. That day when Fernando surprised me with my twin being in America and finally gonna be united with me, was the time I knew, me or Poncho would not ever be able to repay him for his help. Pulling the strings that he pulled was enough in my book to own our, mine and Poncho's loyalty for life.

"Tito is missing and I need the two of you to find him," through menacing eyes, inherited from his long lost father, Fernando said when entering the room.

Dressed wearing a pair of sharkskin grey color slacks, a silk Italian robe, wife beater with his automatic stuffed down the front of his waistline and a pair of $6,000.00 crocodile skin shoes, he looked every bit the part of an underworld player he was.

"Whatever it is, boss," Poncho spoke first.

"Yea, whatever," I concurred.

"You're taking a trip down to Connecticut, to Tito's mother Norma's house. I want you to find Tito, but if not I need my money and cocaine picked up. At Norma's in her basement you will find a fake cement looking wall, behind it you should find two suitcases filled with only money. Over at Tito's condo should be where the bricks are. Here, this is the address to both spots and these are the keys you're gonna need to sneak into Norma's basement," sliding the keys and piece of paper across his desk, Fernando said. "Whatever you find I want it all. Tito was suppose to meet Gomez's dead ass. Gomez claimed he never showed, and that they never did. I didn't believe not one fucking word that thirsty motherfucker had said, and that is why he became food for the gators."

"That's good for em, I didn't like him anyways."

"Me either," Poncho chimed in.

"Yea, my mother needed a treat anyways, just so it had to be a washed-up accountant. That greedy snake had been stealing for years, he thought I didn't know. When I asked him to meet with Tito to pick up and bank the cash, I knew he would try something, now look at him."

Leaning forward and closer to Fernando's desk I was able to see what he'd been looking at the whole time we had been talking. Gomez's mauled by his gators head, wrapped in a clear, plastic bag and sitting on the floor next to him.

Me and Poncho was well known for the crazy shit we did to our victims, but this sick motherfucker Fernando had us fucked up. Keeping Gomez's head for a trophy was too much, but who was gonna tell Fernando that, not me and Poncho. Outside and away from the boss I could tell Poncho had something on his mind.

"What's up bro?" I asked.

"Just thinking about all of Fernando's talk and why he made sure that we saw Gomez's decapitated head."

"What, you're thinking it was intentional or something, like he was sending us a warning?"

"That is just what I'm thinking. I know he was." The look on my brother's face said it all.

"Don't worry, he is going through it right now, I could only imagine how I would be if something like this happened to you how I would be. He will be good when we find and bring Tito back alive," I said trying to change Poncho's mood.

"I guess so," he replied.

Landing at JFK we, Poncho and me, picked up the already rented car waiting for us, after heading straight for Connecticut. Finding Tito's Range Rover sitting in the parking lot adjacent to Norma's, his Mother, huge home looking as good as ever, we was now feeling good about how easy finding Tito had been. Waving Poncho to drive around the back while I get out and see if Tito would answer the door. Receiving no response, we used the key

Fernando gave us to enter the basement as instructed to. "I know that nigga is up there, probably laying up with a nice piece of pussy, not wanting to be fucked with," I said.

"The question is why is he ducking Fernando, that's the million dollar question," the always-thinking Poncho added.

After finding nothing but spots of blood and an already torn down paper cement wall, Poncho and I, me driving now, wheeled the rented Impala through the calm-looking but deadly Bridgeport streets ready to put our murder game down on whoever got in our way of finding Tito.

Dressed wearing different color slacks, button-downs, sport jackets and pair of black leather shoes, Poncho's Gucci, mine off-brand, perfectly fitting in and looking like we belonged there, we moved through the building where Tito's condo was located feeling less confident about finding him alive.

Finding the door cracked told us just what we was already thinking, shit wasn't looking good for finding one of our bosses alive. With our automatics now out and ready to blast on anybody we find in the condo that wasn't Tito, we pushed our way in, Poncho going first with me right on his heels.

Immediately when entering I could smell that there was a noticeable rotten flesh smell coming from the back rooms. Pushing through the ransacked space, we open and entered Tito's bedroom finding him tied down and looking like his face had become a wild dog's mealtime. Leaving me to say a quick prayer over our dead friend and brother's dead body, Poncho walked out of the room to send Fernando the news.

"We found him and it's not good at all" was all that he texted.

DETECTIVE BANKS

"Give me the loot, give me the loot, I'm a bad man," the Notorious B.I.G.'s booming voice blasted out of the club's huge speakers, sending the standing room only packed with ballers from the city and out, there only to stunt, throwing around lots of their green pieces of paper, trying to outshine each other in frenzy, while I sat back waiting and watching Rah-mere and his other Get Down or Lay Down Crew members from across the overly-crowded dance floor.

"Yo son, where's your man? I know if a nigga told me he had twenty-five bricks, and would let them go to me for eighteen-five, he would not be having to wait for me. I would be wherever the fuck he said meet him, before he could even put them shits in a bag. We are giving him 80's prices, shit he wouldn't get unless he took his slow ass across the border and connected with one of them racist-ass Mexicans, and he got us waiting for him." Growing restless Rah-mere was beginning to find it hard to be calm any longer. He hated the club life, unlike Knuckles and other members. Rah-mere was uncomfortable, ready to handle business and get out of there, minutes after they'd walked in.

"He will be here. Why don't you enjoy yourself for once, kick back and have a drink until he get here. You acting like Ayah done gave your ass a curfew or something," Knuckles said, causing laughter amongst the crew and even a smirk from Rah-mere.

"Oh, you a funny nigga tonight, huh? The man with the comedy lines around here. Instead of worrying about Ayah, you need to be worrying about Angie's crazy ass. You keep tricking off with all these trick babies in here, and she's gonna put you and all of your bitches in the dirt. You know she's from where them choppas spray all day, night and year for real, nigga. If I was your Bernie Mack ass, I would put myself on a curfew. Go ahead a laugh at that little nigga."

"Whatever, nigga," Knuckles laughed, stopping the humor short when I walked into their VIP area.

"Look who finally made it, Rah-mere," he said, sticking his hand out to take mine and shake it.

From where he sat Rah-mere said nothing, though his eyes spoke for him, he did not trust me.

Trying to break the ice I stuck my hand out to shake his, yet Rah-mere acted as if he never saw it.

"Great, let's get down to the business," Rah-mere looked to Knuckles, still ignoring me said.

Who the leader of the crew was, that was clear, so shaking the other hands wasn't a part of the mind games I was ready to play.

I had done business with Knuckles a couple times before, so who I was I could tell wasn't the interest of anybody in the team. Getting next to Rah-mere and finding out if they was who's responsible for the killing one week ago of the drug dealer from Florida was my mission, along with a past situation that could possibly haunt me.

"I understand you wanna get down to business, but what would it hurt to have a drink with a business partner, before we get down to it," I said looking into Rah-mere's evil eyes, feeling the same feeling I felt years earlier, looking into his father's.

"We're not your business partners. We have the coke, you have the money, that makes you a customer."

"Okay, I'll give that one to you. Then it wouldn't be a stretch to say, if I'm gonna be spending such a huge amount with you and your team, at least share a bottle of this Lafite Rothchild with me," reaching and grabbing my ordered twenty-three-hundred-dollar bottle of wine from the young curvaceous West Indian bottle service girl, I said.

"I guess we can do that," Knuckles butted in. Handing the girl her tip, five crispy hundred-dollar bills, his attention had been captured by something else.

"While you two enjoy your drinks and try to get to know each other, me, Lefty and Gunem will be right back, I see somebody that needs my attention," Knuckles said leaving me and Rahmere alone.

Viola, one of Knuckle's old flings, a tall shapely white girl with beautiful marble color green-blue eyes, short fire engine red hair and a plump Kardashian-size ass, wearing a tight fitted Chanel skirt that showed off her abs and a pink pair of six inch stiletto heels, conceitedly strutted through the elbow-to-elbow crowded club getting lust-filled comments from club-goers, men and women, wanting to see if she tasted as good as her walk looked. Taking up a spot alongside the dance floor, her and the two other dime pieces she was standing with, Viola waited acting like she didn't notice it was Knuckles, with Lefty and Gunem at his sides walking towards them.

Dressed looking and smelling like new money, Knuckles wore a nicely-tailored Armani suit, his iced out Jesus piece hanging from his neck and a pair of Stacy Adams looking as dapper as the rest of his crew did.

He and Viola had nothing in common but the feeling he had left her with, the last time they'd had sex. The very same feeling that was taking control of her pussy now, making it moist and soaking her thong.

"Long time no see, baby." She pressed her snatch into Knuckles's already hard and feeling like it was gonna burst out of his pants any minute dick, as they shared a tight hug.

"Damn girl! I see you miss me as much as I have missed you." Enjoying the handful of ass he was now caressing and palming, making sure to mark his territory, and show all the other ballers in the club who Viola belonged to.

"Oh yeah, you're rubbing on my ass like I'm on the menu tonight, or let me guess, you've already ate."

"How am I gonna pass on all this pussy? You know I want it right now."

"Well here, smell this, because if you want it tonight you can have it, it's all yours. You know my number." Viola reached down and under her skirt swiping her middle finger over her dripping wet already heater. Rubbing her juices over Knuckles's nose and lips she kissed them all.

Having a clear view from where he sat finishing his drinks with who he thought was a legit buyer, Rah-mere could see Knuckles and who he'd been hugged up with. He believed he'd seen Viola before, but could not place her.

Being able to negotiate a better price for the kilos, four thousand more on each, Rah-mere no longer was in a hurry to get away from me, I was now valuable to him. He had something up his sleeve, and somebody getting laid down was the only thing on Rah-mere's mind, though I didn't know yet.

Returning back to the VIP section from his soft porn show with Viola, Knuckles was now ready to get down to business. While him and Rah-mere spoke, Rah-mere boasting about how he believed he'd talked me into agreeing to pay more on each kilo, I was able to plant my wire where I knew they would be talking, in hopes of picking up some helpful information that'll be useful against them later.

The device was in its position, and now it was time for me to get out of there and away from them. Speaking to Knuckles I let him know that I was ready.

"I'm gonna go and get the money," taking down my last drink, I said.

"And I will meet you at your car with the coke," Knuckles replied.

Speaking to Gunem, Rah-mere gave an order that sent him out of the club, right behind me and Knuckles.

"Be careful, Banks, it's a setup. Rah-mere just gave the order for you to be robbed and killed when you hand over the money," in my ear the undercover detail said, informing me of what he had picked up listening to the planted wire.

Immediately when stepping outside the club, and onto the not-yet-packed sidewalk, my partner, Detective Viola and the very same two beautiful women she'd been with inside the club, also detectives, walked up swiftly passing me my service weapon while acting like they was interested in going home with me.

Taking a couple steps, turning around I came face to face with the truth, a ski mask-wearing Gunem moving fast towards me, Viola and the women brandishing an uzi.

There was only one move to make if I was gonna save my own life, so I made it. Pulling Viola by her arm directly into Gunem's line of fire, at the same time firing my .10 millimeter striking my target down. Standing over and looking down at Viola's still smoking bullet-riddled body, I felt nothing, no remorse at all. It was her laying there or me, and I chose her was what I was thinking. Gunem was down, not moving having taken all eight bullets in his chest and head, and a shocked-looking Knuckles was now out to make me pay for it.

Letting off his first shot from his .357 Desert Eagle in my direction he was knocked backwards, hit square in the chest by a bullet shot from the dark, fired by one of my out of sight men, that left him unconscious and laying right alongside the bag filled with cocaine he'd been carrying.

FERNANDO

Walking into that cathedral seeing Tito's lifeless body laying in that rose gold colored casket, surrounded by all those different arrangements of flowers and hearing the bishop praying over his body really fucked with my head. I have seen many dead people, shit, motherfuckers that I've personally killed or had my men kill, but never my own brother. Traveling down that long marble tile aisle I hoped God would be able to put aside how he felt for me, and allow Tito to hear my promises to him.

"Little brother, I'm gonna miss you. Whoever did this to you best believe I am gonna do everything to find them and make 'em pay for it. And don't you worry about your mother, I'll never leave her, and she'll never want for nothing. Damn man! I really hope you can hear me Tito, I really do," leaning down into the casket, I said in Tito's lifeless ear.

I can't remember the last time I cried, though tears was coming down my face hard now, and I hated it. Stepping back and away from the casket, for the first time I noticed a wearing all black with her face covered with a veil not shedding one tear, and clutching a Santeria figurine of a woman with dry blood on its face, seeking protection over her son's soul as well as placing a curse on the lost ones that killed him, Norma sitting in back of me.

Reaching out with her free hand attempting to console the noticeable to her pain in my eyes, hugging me she whispered, "Find who did this," sending chills over my body.

"I will," was all I could manage to get out.

Pulling from the snow-white Armani suit's pocket I was wearing, I handed Norma her security, an angel wing designed small red box, something I had promised Tito I would do if anything was to of happened to him, before it happened to me.

"This is from Tito. It's ten million which he's saved for this very day. All you gotta do it use the key, the safe deposit box has your name on it. Every dime belongs to you."

"I don't know what to say."

"Whatever it is, say it to your baby, I'll see you later." I kissed the confused-looking Norma on her cheek before leaving, like a general on his way to war.

After praying over Tito's body Norma put the figurine in his cold hands before placing her last kiss on her son's reconstructed face telling him, "Everything will now be okay."

Taking my last look back at Tito and the hurting Norma, I couldn't help but notice the suspicious-looking white man dressed in all black and wearing dark shades, sitting a couple rows away. Was he the Feds, I didn't know and I did not care. All I wanted was to know who killed Tito, so that was all I was determined to get. And I had an idea on how I would.

ORLANDO

My boss said he wasn't sure who took out Tito, though he knew of a few crews that would want him gone being he'd taken over the city, selling the best coke and heroin for cheap. So while Poncho and Pedro do what they gotta do with handling Jamican-Tech, I'm gonna show this sitting duck, G.O. and his friends, just what happens when motherfuckers fuck with us.

Entering Washington Park, mini-fourteen out and ready to tear some shit down, I gave G.O. and his crew no chance to react letting off three quick shots into G.O.'s upper body, never knowing my every move was being watched by statewide officers sitting in an unmarked car across the street.

G.O.'s Carolina blue TSM sweatsuit and all white with blue checks Air Force Ones was now the color of his own blood, and he was no longer moving. Firing at his workers trying to escape my wrath, now running away, "Block, block, blocka" the bullets struck the moving targets knocking both of them face-first into the grass. Seeing them still alive and struggling, I move in for the kill, for I was stopped seeing a gang of yelling for me to put my weapon down undercover cops, pointing their guns at me.

At the very same time I was being arrested, over on East Main and Berkshire Street, Poncho and Pedro had one of Bridgeport's major players boxed in and about to take his last breath.

Pedro driving with Poncho hanging out the window of the stolen SUV, firing until the thirty-two-shot extended clip in his Glock was empty and Jamican-Tech was slumped laying on his CLK's steering wheel, speed away from the scene, leaving the city with another Eastside memory.

DETECTIVE BANKS

How the fuck did we get all these bodies on our hands so fucking fast, partner? This shit don't make any sense. One minute it seems like the city is asleep, and the next minute the place is dropping bodies like they are falling out of the fucking sky. And then we catch that non-speaking English dickhead red-handed getting some street justice, in broad fucking day, using a damn machine gun."

"I don't know, but I'll put my last dollar on it that he's connected to the kid found with his damn face chewed off."

"What makes you say that?"

"I have a strong feeling about it," my soft-spoken, short and plump partner, Detective Darwin said, giving his thoughts some deeper attention.

"It's funny you say that, because when I went by the kid's funeral this morning over at the old cathedral, I noticed that his death definitely did bring out some heavily connected friends."

"Connected, what, like the mob?"

"How else, dim-wick? Yes, like the mob. Actually he's a top player in the Florida underworld, and was down here in Connecticut supplying dealers from here to Chicago, New York, and other cities, all the way up to Canada with pure cocaine and heroin."

"How do you know all this?"

"Hold on, put the lights on," swerving out the way in time enough not to be T-boned by an out of control and moving fast Honda Civic coming directly at us I said, ready to give chase and catch the car.

Trying to get away after robbing a downtown jewelry store, Ya-ya had no intentions to stop for the flashing lights behind him in our Impala's window. Being caught and going to jail wasn't an option, so the chase through the Park City was on. Driving doing whatever he thought it would take to get away, Ya-ya resulted trying to force other drivers off the road hoping we would then back off, yet I continued chasing. I wanted the daredevil bad as fuck now, and I wasn't gonna let up.

Taking a sharp and nasty turn at the bottom of Reservoir Avenue, Ya-ya's NASCAR days was over, crashing into a huge tree.

Driving away from the scene after making sure that Ya-ya was secured in the ambulance and on his way to the hospital, I then finished with telling Darwin about parts of my morning I wanted him to know. "Like I was saying, I went to the kid's funeral, and while I was there a old associate's kid showed up. Don't ask how I know the associate, just know I do."

"That says a lot. Because I do want to know how."

"Look, that dead kid is a partner, is what I know."

"So what are you actually telling me, because it sure sounds like you're saying something without saying all of it."

"What I'm saying is, that death has brought a war to these streets. We got four dead at the park and Rasta-Teck sucking on thirty-two hot ones, shot square in the face. I do not know what that looks like to you, but to me it looks like nothing but retaliation. Somebody wanted them rubbed out, and it got done."

"And how do Tech and them at the park go together?"

"That's what we get paid for, to find out. However they do, is something we need to learn."

"Here, take a look at this, the race car driver from the crash is out of the hospital and now at lockup. Here it says, he's ready to talk," reading the text message on his phone's screen Darwin said.

"That thief haven't even gotten a bond yet, and he is already looking to use a snitch card to get out, let's go and see what he has that we can use."

There was a war that was about to go down, and we needed whatever information we could get. So if this rat wants to talk, you can bet me and Darwin was gonna bring him some cheese.

RAH-MERE

As-salama Alaikam (Peace be on you!)," I greeted Ayah, my wife, finding her standing in our kitchen over the stove cooking dinner.

"Wa Alai-kumus-salam (And on you be peace!)", walking over to hug me she responded, happy to see me. "How was the wake?"

I had just returned from seeing Gunem for the last time, and honestly I felt nothing about it. The look he laid in that coffin with on his face told me everything I needed to know, that he was good, and didn't die afraid of death.

"It was peaceful. He looked really good to be dead. Did you hear from Angie?"

"I did. She was just needing to talk about how that judge refused to give Meelik a bond, even after they shot him. That girl is gonna worry herself crazy about that man," Ayah said, talking about Knuckles' wife.

"Well, what you think you'll be doing if it was me the one that was locked down, and those white folks talking about you can't take me home?" I teased causing Ayah's high yellow skin complexion to turn beet red blushing.

"She did say she was able to visit him. That he's looking better than he was when he first got shot, and all he keep talking about was missing Gunem's funeral."

"She could tell him Al-hamdu-lillah (All praise is due to Allah), that Gunem looked good and we made sure that he was dressed ready for where he's going. And Insha-Allah (if it pleases Allah) our brother will get to see the beautiful garden that awaits us all, so he don't have to worry about him."

"Yes. Insha-Allah. I got a call today. Ya-ya got himself locked up again," changing the subject Ayah said, speaking of her only brother.

Ya-ya was my brother in-law and someone whose problems always became mine as well, having to always get him out of trouble. Him being my wife's only brother I was sure to assure her that I would watch out for him. But now I was feeling good that I didn't have to worry about him, and hearing the reason his careless ass had been placed on lock.

"He can't be bonded out."

"Why?"

"I don't know."

"Okay, so call your mother so that she won't be worrying. Let her know I'll have him out the minute that he could be, Insha-Allah. I'm gonna step out for second, gotta check on Wax. He's been taking Gunem's death real heavy."

"Is he okay?"

"Hope so. I haven't seen him. He didn't show up to the wake. Lefty told me he's been going to see some card and palm reading lady, who told him that somebody has placed a curse on his soul. He also said, when he had went over to Wax's house he found Wax in his garage butt-naked, standing over a human skull with white markings written all over his body and drinking blood from a skeleton goat skull."

"Hu, how did he know it really was blood?"

"He said that brother had the body of a fully grown goat laying surrounded by hundreds of different color glass lit candles. He slit the goat's throat and drunk the damn thing's blood, Ayah."

"Hasbu-Kallah (May Allah suffice thee)," Ayah recited a prayer from the Quran, for her lost Muslim brother.

"I will see you when I get back." I kissed my beautiful concerned for Wax's soul wife on her cheek before heading for the front door, never expecting what happened next.

"Oh shit, get down, Ayah!"

"Boom boom, crash!" The door came crashing in and off the hinges. Grabbing Ayah by the arm I rushed her up the stairs to our room, placing her in the closet, out of harm's way. Ayah was safe, I now had my weapon and was ready to confront my home invaders. Carefully moving softly on my toes, AK-47 with two duct-taped seventy-five round clips together I was out to show whoever it was in my house how they had fucked with the wrong nigga.

Noticing the word Police scrawled across the backs of the Teflon vest wearing undercovers standing in my living room, I ignored them spraying down all three, knowing they was there to kill me and Ayah, not to arrest us.

KNUCKLES

Ihave been locked up in this shitpin for three damn months without a bond, and the whole time I've been here these country-ass Germans has been giving me fucked up looks like I supposed to give a fuck that they're the deepest in here on this yard. Their leader Jose, I hope he don't think I don't know about his connection to that Florida nigga Wax killed. While I'm here I am gonna have to keep a close eye on all of them.

This new cat, I do not know him but I've heard about that work he put in over in the park, smoking G.O.'s fraud ass. I can use him, and I know he can use me while he's here, especially how Jose and his gangsters is moving in this place. When he finishes his workout I'm gonna go over to introduce myself, hopefully he'll understand how him being new on the yard can possibly become a big problem for him if he continued to stand alone. I was willing to be his eyes as long as he was willing to be mine.

"Hey, my friend, what set do you claim?" stepping to Orlando finding him when I was no longer around him, Jose asked.

"Why, who wants to know?" Orlando stopped what he had been doing, ready to show Jose and whoever else on the yard how his thump game was on point.

After agreeing to a peace treaty with me, and me letting him know how Jose and his people rocked, Orlando was ready for whatever the 5'7" muscular built with wavy slick back hair Jose was bringing to him. Orlando had been on the yard for three whole weeks, and not until Jose had seen me and him talking did he make it his business to want to know who he was. So Jose's overdue introduction made Orlando wary.

"It's not like that, bro, I come in peace," speaking in Spanish and showing his hands, Jose said.

"Then what's it like."

"My name is Jose. I run everything on this yard, and Tito, your peoples, I use to do business with him."

"So what, he is dead now."

"Yeah, I know. And I also know that Fernando is down here in CT. looking for who killed him."

"Where would you get information like that from," not feeling how Jose was speaking of business he shouldn't know about, Orlando was growing angry by the second and curious by the minute listening to him.

"That look in your eyes is saying something to me. Let me make it clear to you, you do not have to worry about no snitch or snake shit coming from this end."

"I don't know of a Fernando so I have no worries. Because I do not know what you are talking about."

"Okay, I get you, you don't trust me, but listen to this. Bridgeport is a small place and the streets is talking. I was close enough to your boss to know all about, and how Fernando puts it down when it comes to anybody going against his way of doing things. If he's in Connecticut like my people tells me, I know he is here looking for the snakes or snake that laid his brother out like they did."

"Okay, so what you're connected, I got that, what's the fuck behind door number two, because I can tell there's a reason behind you letting me in on what you know, so spit it out. I gotta get to the showers before rec is called in."

"You're not gonna like this."

"You let me be the judge of that."

"Your boy and his team is who's responsible for killing Tito."

Orlando's baby face looks was now frowned up and his hazel green blue eyes screamed murder. Thinking to his self he was thinking that Jose better not have been fucking with him because he didn't like me.

"Who are you talking about?" he asked expecting nothing to be any different than what he was already thinking.

"The snake you was talking to earlier."

"And how do you know this?"

"Before he got on the yard, there was a kid name Ya-ya here. He is connected to homeboy and their team. They are stick-up boys. All friends, they call themselves The Get Down or Lay Down Boys. The kid Ya-ya, he use to always be bragging about his brother in-law Rah-mere."

"And who is Rah-mere?"

"He's the leader of that crew and homeboy's right-hand man."

"I saw all of them shiesty motherfuckers in the club living it up nights after Tito was found."

"And that tells you that they did it." Orlando's blood was now boiling, tired listening to Jose go on without giving him anything solid that would give him no doubt that Knuckles and his team really did kill Tito.

"The kid Ya-ya made it clear, those motherfuckers did it. I was so sure that he was telling the truth I made the call to Florida already."

"Did you get a answer?"

"To make sure you got this message."

Orlando took the folded card reading the words written in red ink, "Keep that snake close until you hear from somebody." He then knew Jose wasn't only talking but telling the truth. He had to find a way to get closer to me was his only thoughts

DETECTIVE BANKS

"Do you see this bullshit, the judge dismissed all the charges," wide eye staring unable to believe that Rahmere was back on the streets and smiling a big smile, him, his well-known attorney and wife Ayah, standing on the courthouse's steps, speaking to his partner Detective Darwin, Detective Banks said, slamming down the Connecticut Post newspaper on their table.

Sitting here at the very diner, in the same booth me and Loco had sat some years earlier, made me think of how different things now was for a detective like myself, one would call dirty. The shit I got away with back in the day surely I would not get away with these days. Even though shit has changed, I still have to come up with something and that something has to come quick.

"He has a beautiful wife. She makes me think about my Viola," Detective Darwin said, knowing nothing of my thinking. His focus was on Ayah's beauty and how she stood tall by her man, wearing a silk head scarf that allowed only her brown color eyes and high yellow complexion to be seen.

"Hand me my paper because you're thinking about the wrong shit. I did all that work going undercover placing that bug in their VIP section which got the fucking warrant, and the fucking drugs got thrown out. And you're sitting here lusting over that towel head-wearing bitch."

"I'm not lusting, I am just not that invested as you are. Actually I've been trying to figure out why. Why do they, Rah-mere and that Florida dealer Fernando get under your skin like you show that they do. We have worked a lot of cases before, and I've never seen you like you've been."

"I don't know what you think you're seeing. All I know is this motherfucker gunned down three cops. Tell me, is that not enough for you?"

"Yes it is. So what did Fernando do to you? We hardly know anything about the guy."

"Hey, you can feel how you want is all I will say, I know how I feel, and if you're not with me the sidewalk is right out there," pointing towards outside I said frustrated, Darwin had so many damn questions about the beef I had with Rah-mere and Fernando.

The time for him to know wasn't right, and when it comes I will still not let him in on the whole truth.

"That damn thief thinks he's won the battle. Don't you see that look on his face. I'm not gonna give up and you can't on Viola. You gotta remember what they did to her."

Viola was dead because of me, though Darwin didn't know it. After all, somebody had to take those bullets, and it had to be her because it wasn't gonna be me. The look in Darwin's eyes said I had his attention now. He wanted who was responsible for his wife's death, and believed that belonged to Rah-mere and the rest of the Get Down or Lay Down Crew. "I am with you, all I'm saying is if we're gonna get them, scoring on the dirty side will only put them up in the game a little more points than they already is. Just look at that paper."

"But the only way we're gonna get anywhere next to them is, being ready to use some foul plays. I have been in this game twenty-five fucking years longer than you. I've seen too many straight-lace guys like you come and go. What I know is if you do not give, you surely will get. Now with that, I am ready to get out of here," eating my last piece of steak I laid three twenties down on the table before walking away, leaving Darwin still thinking about how his wife, Detective Viola was killed.

Rushing out the diner almost smashing the front door, getting in the Impala, thrusting his iPhone at me out of breath and struggling to complete his sentences, Darwin badly wanted me to see the message he had received.

"What's up now?" I asked.

"You're gonna hate this. Our confidential informant was found hanging ass-naked in his cell with a bashed-in skull."

"How the fuck did they get to Ya-ya in his cell," was all I could think of hearing what Darwin was telling me.

ORLANDO

Ever since Jose told me about Knuckles and his crew being the ones responsible for killing Tito all I have been able to think about is, how was I gonna get next to him. What could I do to get him to trust me like a brother. Coming up with the perfect answer I placed it in play wanting Knuckles, when he returned to the cellblock to find me down on my knees prostrating, making my afternoon Islamic prayer.

"Al-salaam Alaykum," when I was done praying and now standing folding my prayer rug Knuckles said, sporting a big smile. "I knew it was a reason why I started fucking with you."

"Wa-Alai-Kumus-Salam," I greeted back adding to his enthusiasm.

"Why you ain't tell me you're Muslim?"

"Because I just started practicing."

"Al-humdu-lillah. Well check this out. I should be getting out of here in a couple weeks."

"Oh yeah, when did you learn this?"

"Today, I just came back from seeing my overpaid lawyer. He says the judge has agreed to give me a bond."

"That's what's up," I acted to be happy for Knuckles, though I was thinking only about one thing, how I needed to hear from Fernando before his special day comes. If the time to get Knuckles to bite on what I had plan was ever gonna present itself, that time has to be now while I have him believing I'm his Muslim brother. I then went to work sinking my talons into Knuckles like a hawk does its prey.

"For the shit you've told me about how you and your team get down, I know you would want to help me with this little problem my peoples is having," I said.

"What is that? You know if it's about the Franklins then you can count us in."

"It's about more than that. We got a huge shipment of guns coming in, all kinds of them, and they gotta go quick. I am talking about enough to supply the rebels in Syria with."

"And what will me and my crew be doing and how do we get paid for our work?"

"Your access to the streets gives for a perfect place to get rid of them. As for what the help is worth, how about this. Coke is your team's hustle, is what you told me, right. After fucking with my connection you'll never have to worry about how your gonna get or how much of it ever again. I can promise you that."

When I finished talking I could tell by the look in Knuckles' deceiving eyes that he also had but one mission, to get his and crew's hands on the shipment. Loyalty was nowhere in his heart.

"Everything sounds good to me. Tell your people to count us in."

RAH-MERE

I had to do something to catch a rat so I made a call to a couple old friends I knew would lay some cheese down for me, and make my rodent problem go away. When I read them papers with Ya-ya's name on them, informing on me and the team, giving up old and new bodies, that was when I knew he had to go. I knew Ayah, my wife, would be hurt, her and her mother, but fuck all that it was that snitch nigga getting sent on a one-way ticket to hell or me and my whole team to sit in a fucking cell upstate. Death for Ya-ya was chosen, and I had just the man to get it done.

Me and correctional guard R.B., short for Ricky Bones, use to small time hustle together sailing nickels and dimes of weed to anybody that got high. Him and Knuckles never liked each other, although I always liked that he was a loyal person. I always could get him to do some of the craziest things, so it was no shocker when he said yes to paying Ya-ya's snitching ass a visit.

Wearing a fake human skin mask carrying one of the jail's dumbbells in a gym bag, after placing the cameras that faced Ya-ya's cell in another direction, Officer Bones dressed wearing a regular C.O. uniform, walked up opening Ya-ya's cell door, causing Ya-ya to step back as far as he could get in the tight space.

"Chill out. Calm down, I came to help you get out of here. Your sister Ayah paid me a lot of money to make that happen, so get your shit, and let's get out of here."

Ya-ya didn't know whether to believe Officer Bones or not, though he wanted to. Keeping his eyes on the bag he was ready to at least listen to the officer, somebody he did not remember ever seeing around the jail before.

"You're looking at me all crazy, motherfucker you better be ready to get out of this place. Rah-mere wants your head on a platter. I am sure you know this. If you are still here in the morning you're gonna be a dead man."

"Where are you getting all this from?"

"Listen, Ayah knows everything. Now you can stay here and ask all the questions you want. If you want to get out of here you better hurry. I do not give a fuck either way. I can help you out of here, or help them put your dead body in a body bag. One way or the other, I'm gonna get paid what I am owed."

"Okay, let's go, let's get out of here," the convinced, moving now in a hurry Ya-ya said, thinking about his sister ready to do as C.O. Bones wanted him to.

Slipping the dumbbell from the bag, Officer Bones hid it out of view waiting for the perfect opportunity to make his move. Ya-ya was moving around and still talking, when C.O. Bones with every ounce of force in his body drove the ten-pound dumbbell into the back of his head, stopping him in mid sentence.

"I knew my si…," was all he could get out before his lights went out. Face down laying in his own different colors of pus and brains, Ya-ya laid covered in blood and pieces of his smashed skull.

C.O. Bones doing exactly as I'd asked him to, turning Ya-ya's body over, reached into his own shirt pocket pulling out a small piece of paper, written in red ink on it, 'death for all snitches'. Jamming the paper into Ya-ya's stuck and gaping mouth feeling good while doing it, he had one more thing to do. Ripping the sheets from Ya-ya's flimsy cot he placed one end, wrapping it around Ya-ya's neck and the other high on the cell's bars. Pulling until the already dead Ya-ya's lifeless body was hanging, C.O. Bones left him to be found like I wanted.

Wanting Ya-ya to be the example to whoever that thought or was thinking to try bringing me or anybody else in the Get Down or Lay Down Crew down, to know it wouldn't be a comfortable feat, yet the only attention I received came from my closest connection.

As calm as C.O. Bones had walked into Ya-ya's cell he walked out, heading straight for the off-camera spot in the cell block.

Removing his skin mask and changing into a clean uniform he moved with the change of shift in mind, knowing he had to get rid of the bloody murder weapon.

KNUCKLES

I was happy as hell to see Rah-mere walking into the visiting room, especially after Angie had told me what he had said when she told him I wanted him to come visit me.

I needed to talk to Rah-mere about the deal I had already made with Orlando, and it couldn't wait until I got out.

"What is it that couldn't wait two more weeks?" Rah-mere asked as we shared a quick hug and dap.

"Al-Salaam-Alaykum to you too, my nigga. Angie did tell me how you was feeling about coming up here, and wasn't trying to step back in no jail when you did not have to. This isn't that time though."

"We'll see about all that. When Angie said it was about business I knew I had to come."

"So check this out. I got a good lick for us. A real legit one. It'll be some easy paper, unlike some of our old jobs."

"So what are you talking about?"

"You know the kid that smoked G.O. and touched up his peoples, over in the park?"

"The one that got caught red-handed."

"Yeah, him. His name is Orlando, and I got him all lined up right now."

"You know homeboy won't be getting out of here no time soon, don't you," Rah-mere asked confused.

"I do, but it's not him, it is his peoples."

Pushing back from the visiting divider and the center of the table looking like he'd walked straight off a Vanity Fair photo shoot, wearing a perfectly pressed navy-blue Armani suit, a pair of fifteen-hundred dollar Armani loafers, sporting a twelve thousand dollar gold Rolex, Rah-mere getting glances from other prisoners and their visitors asked, "What did you tell him about us?"

"Now you know I didn't do that. What I gave him was nothing but a whole bunch of extra bullshit."

"And how do you know he believes it?"

"He does, I made sure of that. What he did tell me was about his connect, and it's a major one that can use our help."

"To do what?"

"To move a shipment of guns. He tells me it's enough of them, all kinds, to arm a small army. I already agreed that we would be able to take care of it because I know how you think and would want us to be down."

"Bro, you don't ever stop. Do you nigga?" Rah-mere said, smiling and shaking his head at the same time.

"So what do you say, the team is in or what?"

"You checked it out so I'm down. Now check this out. I didn't only come to hear you out, I came to let you in on some work as well."

"I knew your ass wasn't here only because I'd asked you to be."

Whatever Rah-mere was about to tell me I just knew by the look on his face, that look he always gets when he did some serious shit for himself, me or the team, was gonna be something good.

Moving closer to the plastic divider so that I only could hear him he said, "That snitch Ya-ya is dead. I got the word he was talking so I had his trick ass dealt with. Right now he should be hanging in his cell with a cracked skull, like I ordered."

"How did you trap that rat bastard?" I asked, smiling.

"Let's just say I owe a pretty penny to a old friend." Rah-mere's evil sneer told me it was who I thought it was.

"What about Ayah? You know how hard she's gonna take it when she get that call."

"I know, but he was a fucking snitch. She know what he was up against, anybody could have killed his bitch ass," nonchalantly Rah-mere replied.

I could tell it was something that was on my brother's mind. Ya-ya was a rat but still his wife's little brother.

"I know you'll figure it all out, you always do. That coward got what he needed. I wish I could've been the one to do his bitch ass in. Here, take this, it's the number you are going to have to call to connect with Orlando's plug. They'll know who you are when you do," I said, slipping the number over the divider before the C.O. could turn back around and catch me.

Slipping the paper into his pants pocket now standing up ready to walk towards the exit, Rah-mere never knowing when he makes the phone call to the connect it will be the signal needed, Orlando was waiting for, to end my life and the beginning of the end of the Get Down or Lay Down Boyz. Hugging me before leaving he said, "I can't wait to see you free," leaving me feeling the same way.

PART #2

THE BEGINNING OF THE END

FERNANDO

Orlando has been doing some real good work getting and staying close to Knuckles while waiting for me to get back to him. Receiving the call from Knuckles' lawyer that he would be getting out in the next week brought me a sense of satisfaction, knowing when my message had reached Orlando's hands surely one of Tito's killers would get just what he deserves.

Why was there a C.O. looking in at him and not saying anything, was what Orlando was thinking as he stared back, waiting for the metal door to be popped open. Clutching the piece of sharpened titanium he always had on him, never going anywhere without it, he was ready to use it if he had to.

When the hulky speaking Spanish looking guard signaled wanting his cell door popped, gripping the shank Orlando was ready to shake the prison, until he was stopped hearing my name.

"You are Fernando's peoples."

"Yeah, that's me." A relaxed but still holding onto his piece Orlando answered, stepping to the 6'7" and built like a football player looking officer, now standing in his cell.

"So am I. I was sent to give you this, and if you need my help with anything else just let me know, we're family," he said delivering my message.

The new connection was gone and Orlando couldn't wait to read what I had sent him. Tearing into the envelope he was careful not to rip the main attraction inside of it.

"The Connection" was the only words I wanted Orlando to have, that gave him the verification, Rah-mere had indeed made the call and the connection with Knuckles' crew was on.

"The plan's going perfect, just how I expected," Orlando told his self now prepared to checkmate Knuckles.

I had been waiting to hear from Rah-mere, and actually thought he had a change of mind and wasn't gonna call. When he finally did it was not like I was filled with hate and sitting on the other side of the phone listening to him. For some weird reason, hearing his voice it made me feel something I never felt before, though I couldn't figure out what it was I had been feeling. He was one who had killed Tito, yet I wasn't feeling any hate at all towards him.

"Why am I feeling like this, like I care for this thief," I asked myself, not feeling like my normal not giving a fuck self. My cold heart had been experiencing love, something it hadn't since losing my mother, and I couldn't control it.

Orlando's plan was going as good as it could have been. Knuckles was believing he was his equal, a loyal Muslim brother, and he and his crew was about to strike it big. He had one more thing that had to be done, and Orlando was going to make sure that it was.

"Al-Salaam-Alaykum," showing up at Knuckles' cell, finding him getting ready for Jum'ah (the Friday Muslim prayer service), Orlando greeted Knuckles.

"Wa-Alai-Kumus-Salam," Knuckles greeted Orlando back, happy to see him.

"What's got you smiling like that, Auk?"

"Because I'm happy. Did they make it a felony if Knuckles smiled around here?"

"No, brother, they didn't do that. But you're smiling like I'm gonna be when them white folks set my black ass free."

"All praise due to that."

"But did you hear they canceled services today."

"I didn't, I was at work."

"Yeah, they did, I came over here to let you know and to tell you your man made the connection. I got the word today." Feeling the knife sliding down his pants leg, he caught it before allowing it to hit the ground. As Orlando's moves on his chess board was looking promising to him Knuckles was feeling the same about his. Everything was right on track was Knuckles' thinking.

"I guess all is well then. I knew he would. I just can't wait to get out of here with him, this last week seem like it's taking forever to end."

"I bet you can't wait. It's time for prayer, we can talk about it all after."

"Where do you want to do it?"

"We could do it over on the other side you know right where we did it before."

"Over there on Jose's side, you know I hate seeing that crab."

"You need to chill with all that. Fuck him and whoever else. Today is Allah's day and that's what we're gonna go over there for."

"You are right, I'm down. Let me get my prayer rug," Knuckles said blindly being led into a death trap.

Walking past Jose and his crew, he and Knuckles, using his prayer rug to conceal the bulge at his right side, Orlando made sure that Knuckles saw how he gave Jose his hardest murderous stare. Having been the one to plant the seed that Knuckles and his team had been responsible for murdering Tito, Jose watching giving his hardest look back, playing his part, as Orlando herded Knuckles like herdsman do their flock towards his last days.

Orlando and Knuckles had been in the middle of completing their prayers bending over, hand on their knees in the prostrating position of Ruku, when knuckle's body crashed down to the floor face first, feeling pain shooting through the center of his back.

Sneaking up, driving his sword sized shank into Knuckles' back, Jose took pleasure finally getting to plunge his steel into Knuckles' flesh.

Knuckles laid face down on his blood-soaked rug, Orlando was nowhere around and Jose still using his bloody knife, continued his assault, wanting his victim not breathing. Praying, begging Allah for mercy was all Knuckles could do, hoping his prayer was heard while Jose relentlessly treated his body like a butcher does fresh meat.

AYAH

"He's dead, he's dead, they killed him, Ayah!"

"Wait a minute, Angie, slow down, who's dead? What are you talking about?"

"They killed him. Them bastards fucking killed him," was all Angie could manager to get out through the uncontrollable sobbing.

"Please! Try to calm down. Just take a few deep breaths."

"I can't believe it, Meelik is gone. He is gone. He ain't never coming back to me, Ayah. He was all that we have."

First I had to spend the last couple days helping my mother get ready for my little brother Ya-ya's funeral, and now here's my best friend telling me her husband is dead.

Knuckles was supposed to come home next week.

I hadn't seen or heard from Rah-mere in some days, so now I was starting to worry that something had happened to him as well. Saying a silent prayer to myself I begged Allah while still listening to my broken-hearted Muslim sister. "Please, All Mighty! Watch over my husband, don't let Rah-mere be dead."

"Are the girls up?" I asked Angie.

"NO," she answered between breaths and quietly sobbing.

"Where in the house are you?"

"Down in Meelik's TV room. Them girls are going to be crushed, Ayah. You know how they feel about their daddy, they're going to be hurt. I cannot believe this, he only had another week to come home to us, one more fucking week."

"Yes, Sister, I know, but now you have to be strong for your girls. They're going to need all of your strength right now. So you're gonna have to pull it together and be there for them because they can't do it for their selves. I know how you must feel, but you must remember that Allah is the planner of all things. Growing up the way you did, and living the life you was forced to before you got to this country tells me that there's nothing you can't handle."

"I know, Ayah, I know," no longer sobbing, intently listening hanging on to my every words, Angie replied.

"I want you to know whatever you and the girls need, me and Rah-mere are going to always be here for ya'll. Your lost is ours. So girl, get yourself together before them girls come down them stairs on you."

"I'm sorry, Ayah, I know you're still going through what happened to Ya-ya."

"Listen, your husband is my brother as well. I know Allah has them both. And whoever did or had this done to them will surely get what they got coming to them, so I have no worries."

"Oh, I cannot wait, I can't wait for the day to come."

"You go and get them girls up and come over here, I'm going to call Rah-mere. He's going to lose his damn mind when I tell him his brother is dead."

"I will do that and be right over there."

Dialing Rah-mere's number I got his voicemail which made my heart shake, and the thoughts that was already in my head even more reliable.

Rah-mere had always been sure to check in with me whenever he wouldn't be making it home in time for a salat or dinner, this was nothing like him. Whatever it was, Ayah refused to believe that Rah-mere was dead.

Texting what she believed would get a quick response from Rah-mere, "Our Brother Meelik has gone home to the Creator, may Allah have mercy on his soul," she waited hoping he text her back and put her worries out of her heart.

DETECTIVE BANKS

"I don't know what's going on, but surely something big has happened or about to," listening to another one of my illegal wiretaps hearing J.O. talking, I informed Detective Darwin, sitting at his desk across from me in our not so spacious office.

"What makes you say that," he asked taking a break from reading one of the books his deceased wife use to rave about, A Black Girl's Worth.

"Because these recordings are telling me that. What I haven't heard in any of them is one word about Knuckles' or Meelik's, whatever name you wanna use for that dead asshole's death."

"How do you take that for something big is about to go down?"

"If you put that fucking book down maybe you will be able to see the significant facts. The Get Down or Lay Down Crew have been talking less than they've ever did before. No revenge talk no nothing. The obvious code here is silence, and you know what they say about how bad boys move."

"You know what partner, you might just be on to something. And you haven't gotten anything from the wire you have on Rah-mere's phone."

"Nothing. I believe the son of a bitch is using one of those high-power satellite blockers, that prevents any kind of tapping in on his line. How did he get it, I do not know, but he had to have paid a nice amount for it, and to some serious connected people."

"Definitely, some government type because that's some shit only they can get their hands on. What about the wives, what have you gotten from them?"

"The same oh shit, Rah-mere's wife talking about her brother and Abraham's crying about losing hers. Both of them Muslim bitches need a stiff drink and some hard cock."

"You're a cold man, partner."

"I did pick up that Rah-mere hasn't been in contact with either one of them, in some days. I could see him not contacting Angie."

"Who?"

"Knuckles' wife, Abraham, whatever the scumbag's name is. But that's her name. I can see Rah-mere not contacting her, but not one call to his wife. Something tells me a dead fish is stinking somewhere."

"Here, come check this out," pointing to his iPhone's screen Detective Darwin said, wanting to show me something he'd been working on.

"What the fuck!" I reacted, reading twice what he was showing me. A connection Darwin had down south in Texas at one of the coroners' offices and the homicide unit out of Dallas was informing him that Pain and Lefty, two members of the Get Down or Lay Down Crew had been murdered. I could not believe what I was seeing.

"And you thought you was the only one working," Darwin said, smiling that same look he always use when he knows his work has shocked me.

"I admit, this is some good work. This is huge news. I would bet my last dollar on it, this is the happening I've been talking about." I handed my partner his phone back.

Minutes after Detective Darwin had received his phone it pinged, sending notice he was receiving another message.

"Here's the answer to your questions," he said reading the text out loud to me.

"Pain and Lefty was ambushed and found dead with ten crates of unworkable machine guns." The mystery to what Rah-mere and his crew was up to came like music to my ears.

"Now the question is where's that sick motherfucker they call Wax. This tells us, Rah-mere and J.O. both are alive."

"While you figure that out, Columbo, I am going for a coffee. Would you like one?" Darwin poked.

"Fuck you asshole!" I responded.

There was two more moves I believed I need to make, though the first was one I never knew would have to be made.

Picking up my desk phone, I dialed a old friend's number. Hearing the voice on the other end of the line immediately brought back twenty-three-year-old memories.

RAH-MERE

Pain and Lefty was dead, set up by Orlando's people, Florida niggas I see now was out for revenge on all of us for laying one of their bosses, Tito down. I still cannot believe Knuckles fell for that nigga's game. He let Orlando get next to him and the whole time the angle was to body every one of us. "Damn! My brother may your soul rest in peace. I will deal with these niggas and get revenge for you, Lefty and Pain, I just wish you wouldn't have trust 'em," I was thinking to myself as me and J.O. waited for Fernando and his goons to show, at the same time I thought about where Wax was.

Listening to the voices in his head telling him what to do and how to do it, Wax was on a mission to confront the demons that was controlling him, moving like a venomous snake across his soon to be victim's property.

Tip-toeing moving cat-like he scurried over the eight-bedroom Victorian home floors, causing a occasional screeching noise. Wax's nose had been constantly bleeding and his hearing had been lost, which only started when finding out that he'd been cursed. He was now out to stop it, listening to the demons chattering non-stop as they guided him towards the responsible target. The 27-306 jacket he was wearing was now soaked in his blood, being Wax held it to his face trying to stop the bleeding. His automatic ready and in hand, Wax climb the house's two flights of stairs in search of the devil.

When reaching the very top and very last step, he was knocked backwards having to grab onto a attached railing to catch his balance by a violently moving past him shadow.

Rushing now back up the stairs while pointing his Glock "19" directly at the master bedroom where he was sure the shadow had come out of, a confused Wax understood nothing the voices now was telling him to do, for they were no longer understandable, talking all at the same time sounding as if they was speaking in tongues.

Following the silhouette showing on the high ceiling walls he entered the lit up by candles space, finding the elderly, frail and weak-looking Norma down on her knees surrounded by candles and figurines, alongside her huge mahogany wooden color canopy bed that took up most of the space in the room.

Worshipping to her Santeria gods holding in her hands a human skull in the left and a animal skull in the right, startling Wax who stepped back still with his gun pointed at the back of her head when she began welcoming him without ever turning around to see who it was, and same time pouring from the two skulls, blood that she smeared herself in Norma said, "Welcome, I am glad you could make it. You are the evil soul that mutilated my son. I have been waiting for your arrival. Thank you for bringing your soul as payment. Today is the day you will pay."

Squeezing the trigger, Wax's Glock didn't fire, nor did it jam. Knocked out his hand by an unknown force, the weapon was sent flying across the room, the candles had been blown out rendering pitch darkness and no more worries.

When the lights had come back on Wax was laying dead on his side with maggots, worms, blood and green pus coming out of every hold on his head, while Norma laid right beside him, her body being wrapped and crushed by a twenty-three-foot-long python, readying her for its dinner.

RAH-MERE

"Do you see anything on that side," crouching down in my position, in one of Fernando's Florida warehouses I called out to J.O.

"I don't see his white limo down there, only a couple of goons," he answered, speaking of Fernando and the limousine our kidnapped informants said he would be riding in.

The old rundown, once a factory, building sat on seventy-five acres of farmland located deep in the Tallahassee woods miles away from any main roads. This made for a perfect spot to knock off Fernando and all his goons at the same time, and never have to worry about any of them. I just hope everything is good with Wax I thought to myself, unaware that he'd already went up against his demons and lost.

"It should be here any minute, keep your target on them," having crawled over to where J.O. was, now looking through the scope on my rifle down at the congregating, getting ready for something goons.

Reflecting back on everything that brought me and J.O. to Tallahassee, I thought back to the day I'd let Knuckles convince me to meet and do some work with and for Fernando's people. "I can't believe I agreed to do it. They outsmarted me," I told myself.

Panama, one of Fernando's lieutenant, had agreed to what I believed was a sweet deal, on top of my ultimate mission that involved Lefty and Pain ending up with everything turned out to be nothing but a big trap and major mistake.

"I can't believe it," I said, recognizing how I'd been outsmarted and played, at the very game I figured I was the master of. Pain and Lefty was to transport the guns to Texas from Florida, and the team would get ten kilos of pure uncut coke and a crate of AR-15's. The second we had agreed was when Panama's plan was completed and activated.

"It's here," seeing Fernando's limo entering the back side of the building with two goons holding machines guns walking along both sides of it J.O. said, snapping me out of my deep thoughts. Cocking my S.K. it was time to get some payback.

Staying as close as we could to the warehouse's old, dusty, and dingy tile walls, getting closer to our targets, me and J.O. was now only feet away from who we believed was Fernando, standing and giving orders outside of the limousine.

Firing my first three shots, and J.O. his four, dropping the goons before they could raise their guns to fire back we was forced to take cover, and fight off what seemed to be a army of soldiers now firing in our direction.

The goons had no clue where J.O. and I actually was at in the huge space, firing through walls and at closed doors hoping to get their man.

Using my advantage while J.O. struck each soldier down from his position, one by one, I moved in to finish what my first squeeze of my trigger didn't do.

"Look out!" J.O. yelled out seeing Poncho and Pedro readying to shoot, while running up on my blind side.

Diving out of the way in time I saw Poncho spin around and Poncho get stopped in his tracks being showered with bullets.

"That was close," I thought. The expensive white suit was now a bloody red suit with the target down on his side, refusing to stay down on the ground. We had Fernando right where we wanted him, I believed. The back-and-forth shooting had stopped, J.O. was no longer in the protected spot he had been in now standing alongside me with his nickel-plated .45 in his hand, prepared as I was ready to get revenge for our brothers.

Dropping his weapon grabbing at his neck, struck with a bullet fired by Panama from across the warehouse, rage overtook my body seeing J.O. slump to the ground struggling to breathe.

"Hold on, bro, come on, don't do this to me," was all I could say to my falling comrade noticing his fear of death in his eyes.

J.O. was still alive and so was Diablo, the Mexican Boss, Fernando had used to have his men kill Lefty and Pain. Convincing Diablo to ride in his white limousine and attend a meeting at his Florida warehouse, looking to kill two birds with one stone, Diablo did and now was fighting for his life. If I was ever going to get J.O. out of here, and to a hospital I knew I had to locate the M-16 shooting goon. Seeing movement at one of the top levels I engaged rapidly firing back at Panama, hitting nothing but the walls and the light fixtures. Ducking, almost being struck by one of his whistling past my head bullets, I could see the once white suit-wearing Diablo was now on his feet and readying his self to relieve the still-alive J.O., of all his pain. Rapidly I fired hitting the Mexican leader ripping half his head off, believing I was finally done with Fernando forever.

On my way out of the warehouse, trying to get back to the getaway car with J.O. slung over one shoulder and my rifle in the other, I expected another gun fight with the relentless Panama. I had to get J.O. out of there, and I was determined to do so. "Just hold on," I told him, though I knew shit was looking dark for him.

"What the fuck?" I yelled dropping J.O. to the dirt face-first when Panama fired, hitting me in the back of the leg.

Listening I could hear Panama coming, moving like a lion does when he knows he's wounded his soon-to-be food. On my back laying still on the ground, I fired at the sound of his approaching footsteps causing Panama to take cover, buying time to get up off the ground and try getting the looking like he couldn't take anymore J.O. into the car. "You can't give up J.O., I got you," I said, after feeling his body tensely seize up when Panama fired a kill shot sending his brains all over my face.

The pain at my leg was telling me staying behind with J.O. might not've been so bad, but my heart refused to allow it, for I knew I had to make it home to Ayah.

Scurrying into the still-running BMW mashing on the gas pedal, staying low while Panama fired continuously without ever hitting the car, I pulled away from the farmland never looking back, and in search of the nearest interstate sign that pointed me towards I-95 North.

The very time I was doing my best to endure the pain and keep the bleeding from continuing to flow from my wounded leg, a disappointed thinking it was me at the door Ayah was being confronted by a visitor who'd I never did get around to making sure that he'd been paid for his help in being my exterminator.

Handing Ayah a manila envelope, inside pictures of her little brother Ya-ya as he hung in his cell, C.O. Ricky Bones said before walking away leaving her shocked and in tears, "Your husband ordered and didn't pay."

DETECTIVE BANKS

I wasn't hearing J.O. talking on the wire I had on his phone anymore, bodies was still dropping in the city, Rah-mere it seemed had fell off the earth and his brother, Dominican Fernando was out of control ordering murders all over the state, making sure that whoever he knew that was connected to the Get Down or Lay Down Crew was no longer alive. I never thought that I would have to put my first plan in play, but I did, now I had to activate my second, which would assure that the first do as I wanted.

Trying to bring down Fernando and Rah-mere has been nothing like when I'd forced their father out and away from the country. Fernando, a deadly boss player not easy to get next to and Rah-mere, the ever so chess player, if you slip up he'll checkmate you in a couple quick moves.

When I started out twenty-three years earlier it was all about the money, the power and being the baddest motherfucker on the force, until now having my past reveal itself.

My partner, Detective Darwin, lately had been showing more interest in helping me find and lock up Rah-mere and Fernando hoping that they would pay for his wife's death. I need him to get my next move done, so using Viola and his vulnerability will be just what I'll do, to implicate my next move.

"Partner, I don't like mentioning this because I know how you feel about it, but I have a plan and I need to know if you're in with me or not."

"Well, you haven't said anything yet," taking the seat in front of my desk, Detective Darwin replied.

"I have a plan that I believe will work, in getting those cowards for murdering Viola."

"If that's what you're talking about then yes, I'm in. I am ready for whatever that needs to be done to catch those bastards."

"Are you sure?" Pulling a pair of plane tickets from my desk I held them up for Darwin to see them.

"Viola was my wife and they took her away from me, so I am sure. What are those?" Looking up at the tickets still in my hands and then at me Darwin asked.

"They are tickets."

"I can see that, what are they for?"

"They are a part of the plan. Darwin, my problem with Fernando and Rah-mere is deeper than you know. You may want to see them in a cell doing time, I have to see them dead and no longer breathing."

"Have to." I could see on Darwin's face he was regretting ever giving his word, though he knew he couldn't take it back. He was starting to see that I was far from the honorable detective he thought he was partnered with, and closer to the criminals he had signed up to put away. "I got you, your secret is safe with me," he said taking the tickets.

"Great, that's exactly what I wanted to hear. You're on your way to Todos Santos. You shouldn't look so shocked," I said, seeing the expression on Darwin's face.

"It's, I don't even know where that is."

"You're going to love it. It's a beautiful island. The place is gorgeous, blue water, white sand and the pussy out there is different too, everything on the island is. It is located at the southern part of the Baja Peninsula, right off the coast of Mexico. You shouldn't stand here and keep asking so many questions because your flight takes off tonight, so you got to go and get yourself ready."

"Tonight?"

"Yes, tonight, Viola would not want us to wait any longer."

RAH-MERE

Making it home after thinking I might not, and would be found on the side of the road having bled to death, finding Ayah seemingly not as happy to see me as I was to see her really weighed on my mind, but I was in pain and had no strength to find out why. All I wanted was for her to do is stitch me up, give me something for the pain and let me rest. Whatever it was I knew could wait, and be dealt with later.

After stitching me up and helping me into bed she was ready to make a call to her mother that she knew was against what she believed, but had to be done.

"Al-Salaam Alaykum, mommy."

"Alaykum Salaam, baby. What's wrong, why do you sound like that Ayah?"

"Oh, it's nothing, momma."

"Girl, do not give me that. The only time your voice gets that raspy is when you've been crying. You know your momma know, so talk to me, talk to momma baby."

"I'm just calling to ask if I could come home," her voice starting to crack, Ayah said.

"Of course you can. This will always be your home, Ayah. You don't have to ask me that. All you got to do is bring your butt down here. What happened, did Rah-mere put his hands on you?"

"No momma, he didn't. Now, I don't want you worrying about me."

"Well, you're all I have left. Ever since your brother was killed all I have been doing is worrying about you. You are my last child, so not worrying I don' t know how to do that anymore."

Listening to her mother speak of losing her brother, and knowing that it was by the hands of her husband caused hate to take the place of the love Ayah had in her heart for Rah-mere. He was a enemy and sleeping upstairs in her bed.

"I won't promise to not worry. If I did I would be telling a fib. But I will say, just bring yourself home, I'll be waiting for you."

"Okay momma, I will," silently crying with tears running down her face, Ayah said thinking only about how Rah-mere betrayed her.

"He knew how I felt about Ya-ya. Ya-ya was my only brother, and he had him killed," Ayah told herself convinced her husband had to die, just like her brother did.

When I'd showed Ayah where she would find my extra weapon in case of a emergency, I never thought she would one day be contemplating on using it on me.

Ayah's hands were trembling and her mind was made up. Digging down into the open space at the side wall behind the fixed and mounted on the wall seventy-two inch flat screen, Ayah fiddled around in the narrow space until she felt the cold piece of iron, a old rusty-looking rubber grip thirty-eight long.

Thinking to herself how she would get away with killing Rah-mere, for every cop in the city and mayor would love to see him under the dirt and no longer dropping bodies in the city, Ayah felt no regrets for what she was only minutes away from doing. Concealing the revolver under the emerald green-color hijab she was wearing, Ayah was heading up the stairs to where Rah-mere still laid sleeping, stopping when hearing noise she thought coming from the back of the house. She headed back down the circular style stairs to investigate.

Finding nothing, she contributed what she thought she'd heard to her own nerves, "You gotta calm down Ayah," she spoke telling herself.

I was still laying in pitch darkness and feeling drowsy from the wearing off medication when Ayah walked into the room, pulling back the blacking out all sunlight drapes.

"You killed my brother. I can't believe you, Rah-mere, you had him killed," pulling the pistol from under her hijab, Ayah said pointing the gun at me. Her face was covered in tears, her voice as raspy as I've ever heard it and when looking into her eyes the only thing I saw was murderous thoughts. "Ayah, honey, that's not true. Please! Don't let this division by the devil to be the death of us," pleading with my wife I said, hoping she would lower the gun.

"You are the worst kind of person, Rah-mere. You're a fucking liar. You lied to me, you gave me your garbage bag word, and that is all it was, fucking garbage. Ya-ya was murdered like a dog, and I am now going to watch you lay there and die like one," squeezing the trigger watching her first bullet enter my chest Ayah said smiling.

Wishing that she had done a better check of the downstairs, Ayah thoughts proved to be true hearing another gun go off, stopping her before she could fire again. Thrown across the bed and now laying on top of the not moving Rah-mere, with the back of her head blown off, Ayah had finally made it to the afterlife.

DETECTIVE BANKS

Rah-mere and Fernando's war against each other had become too much for me to go on trying to stop, so I figured to call in somebody that might could help. The situation needed a wicked play, so I sent Detective Darwin and some help to make it.

Parked sitting him and Velez, someone that lived on the island, and I had sent to be sure everything went as planned, sat in a tinted window van on a Todos Santos street, across from Loco's thirteen-year-old daughter, Amanda's school, Detective Darwin hated that he let me trick him into doing what him and Velez was about to do.

Snatching Amanda off the streets I knew would get Loco to return, and do as I wanted him to. Velez was the opposite of Detective Darwin, though a professional at kidnappings, so I knew he would get it done just how I needed it to be.

"Why are you sweating so hard," recognizing the beads of sweat on Detective Darwin's forehead, Velez sarcastically poked. "That's her right there," he said, leaping out of the van with a black sheet in hand before Darwin could say a word.

Throwing the sheet over Amanda's head engulfing her whole 5'2" and petite body, he dragged her kicking and screaming into the back of the van.

Hours had gone by, Amanda was now where I wanted her to be, locked in one of the rooms in my vacation cottage located deep on the island, no longer covered with the sheet or wearing a blindfold over her eyes. Although her hands was still tied they were in front of her, and not behind like Velez had first did.

"Calm down, we're not here to hurt you. You can trust me," speaking to Amanda Detective Darwin said, same time thinking of his wife and what their family could've looked like. He couldn't take it anymore, he wanted out, so he found a good connection to call and let me know just how he was feeling.

"I am done, I'm fucking done, man! We got the girl like you wanted, now I want out! I want off this fucking island!" Darwin was sounding like he was losing his sanity.

"You can't quit just yet, Darwin, the show just started. I need you to give me two more days, and I will be down there. That is all I'm asking you for, just give me that."

"Banks, all that sounds good but this isn't what I signed up for. This is your shit, not my kind."

"Actually, you did," I shot back tired of hearing my partner complaining. "You should see it like this, all of this is not only for me, it's for Viola and getting who killed her. All of what we are doing is for you as well, and don't you forget it," sticking my pitchfork deeper, I knew I had again struck Darwin's weak spot.

FERNANDO

Jose was out and ready to accept his reward for doing away with Knuckles, as I ordered Orlando to hire him and his peoples to do. Today would be the day I would introduce him to all the major crime bosses, which I had come together so that he could officially be inducted into our family, and be forever known as a made man from Connecticut.

Jose made sure that Knuckles paid for Tito's death, so it was only right that I allowed him to control all of Tito's businesses. Walking with a strut that made him feel like he was the baddest motherfucker alive, on his way to meet his new associates, dressed wearing a perfectly tailored Versace suit, a pair of Red Bottoms and his Glock 40 at his waistline Jose headed to his sitting on twenty-two inch rims Range Rover, never knowing what awaited him lingering in the dark.

Dressed laying on the sidewalk next to where Jose had parked, looking like one of the many bums in the city and listening to the sound of Jose's Red Bottoms clicking against the asphalt coming towards him, a heavier, salt-and-pepper-color goatee, long dreadlocks that hung down covering the front of his dirty-looking face, Loco concealed his .40 caliber in a paper bag, acting as if it was a cheap bottle of wine.

Jumping up off the ground the paper bag no longer covering the bulky .45 he held in his hand, now pressing it against the side of Jose's face, Loco managed to catch Jose off guard as he tried walking by, as if he never saw him sprawled out drunkenly acting on the ground.

"Don't move. Where is the gate opener? I know you have it so do not play with me," In a deep Mexican-sounding accent Loco said, wanting the gate opener that would get him onto my compound without being detected.

"Take the money, it's five thousand t…" holding his hands over his head Jose said, acting as if he didn't know what the shabby-looking Mexican was talking about. If it was money he wanted he could have it, but giving up my loyalty he was prepared to die for, was what Jose was thinking.

"Get in the truck," not wanting to be seen Loco forced Jose into the driver seat of the Range, never taking his automatic off him. Taking the back seat directly behind Jose, having screwed a silencer onto his weapon placing it against the back of Jose's head, Loco became disgusted with how quick Jose's loyalty for me, his son, changed. Jose did not want to die so it was fuck me. "Here take it, you can have it, it's right here," Jose rambled looking to make it out of the luxury ride alive, yet little did he know Loco hated disloyal soldiers, especially ones that showed disloyalty to a son of his he'd yet to meet.

Jose wasn't willing to die for protecting me as Loco believed he should've been, so now he had to go. Placing the silencer to the back of Jose's head he pulled the trigger putting five hollow points in Jose's skull, painting the Rover's windshield and dashboard with his brains, leaving a strong stench of burnt hair and gunpowder in the air.

Exiting the back seat now back standing on the sidewalk, hunched over and calmly walking over to a waiting shopping cart filled with bottles, soda cans, and other homeless-looking props,

Loco slowly walked away blending into the night with everybody else that was out, and going about their life.

DETECTIVE BANKS

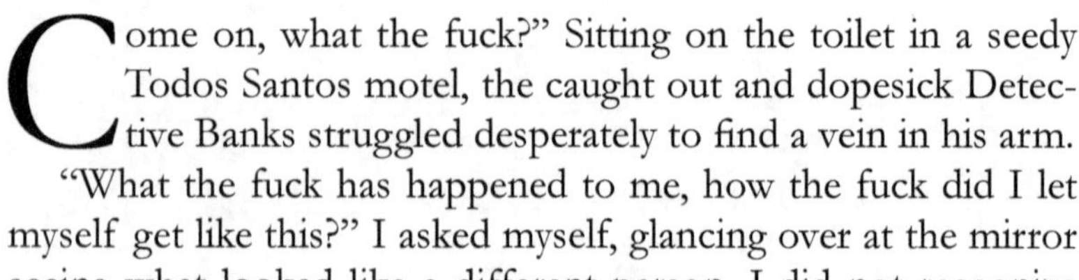

ome on, what the fuck?" Sitting on the toilet in a seedy Todos Santos motel, the caught out and dopesick Detective Banks struggled desperately to find a vein in his arm.

"What the fuck has happened to me, how the fuck did I let myself get like this?" I asked myself, glancing over at the mirror seeing what looked like a different person. I did not recognize who was looking back. What I was looking at was somebody who was looking like every other heroin and crack addict hanging out hustling right outside in the parking lot, and I hated it.

Hearing Loco's voice after so long, and the chilly sound in it when he promised that he would kill me if I touched one hair on his daughter's head, really did something to me. I had always sniffed dope but never have I ever shot it into my arms, and here I was now trying to not think of what the future can look like. I know one thing, Darwin and Velez has Amanda locked away, and if Loco gets out of line, just like I told him I'll order them to cut that little bitch's head off her shoulders.

"Aghhhhhh!" Out of the bathroom and now standing in the disheveled room were my opened suitcase and everything that was in it laid flung all over the place, the heroin was doing as it always does, erasing all my worries.

Downing the leftover glass of scotch left sitting on the stand next to the bed, I was ready to go and meet Darwin and Velez.

Pulling up to the lone vacation home on the deep country side of the island I thought about everything that brought me there. First, how I learned about Loco and the load he would be carrying how I followed Loco into the city and out after relieving him of his stash, then forcing him to exile to Mexico and now making him come back to stop his own sons. Now I have his little princess inside holding her for negotiating power. Until I get something that tells me Loco has done as I called him back to do, I will hold onto her, no matter how long it takes.

"Where's Darwin?" Entering the home seeing only Velez and no sign of my partner or Amanda, I asked the AK-47 slung over his back Velez. "How's the girl doing?"

"She won't eat a thing. She's tied up in the back room. And man, what the fuck is up with that fucking nutcase partner of yours, you sent me to watch over? All he's been talking about, repeating over and over, something about you killing or getting his wife killed. I swear, he done lost it," in his deep island accent Velez shaking his head said, as we walked towards where Detective Darwin was and haven't left since the last time we'd spoke.

Walking back and forth in the reeking of feces room, a smell that bothered my already compromised by the heroin system, looking in at Detective Darwin from the open doorway, for the first time in a long time I felt regret for pushing him so hard as I did. I always knew he wasn't built for any of it, yet I didn't know he would end up like this. Staring into Darwin's eyes I could tell the person I'd spoken to days earlier, and the partner I once knew would never be the same.

"Darwin, come on, it's over partner," moving in closer I said, though only received a empty stare. The look in Darwin's bloodshot red eyes was one I had never witnessed before. Shrugging, raising his shoulders up and down expressing his uncertainty he continued to walk the piss and shit covered floors, showing no sign that he knew I was there or what I was there for.

"You see what I was saying, this retarded fuck, if you want I'll put one in his stupid head," Velez said, pulling his .357 from its holster.

"You let me worry about him, and you go and get the girl ready to move out of here, that's what you can do for me," I was tired of hearing Velez's complaining, plus, looking at my phone brought a great feeling of happiness. I received a message that said, Rah-mere and Fernando both are no longer breathing. I did what you wanted, so now it's time to let my little girl go. I'll pick her up where you said to be. I could not believe what I was reading. The time to celebrate was now, waiting until I released the girl wasn't gonna do it being the monkey on my back was now showing its head needing a fix.

The heroin was drained and in the syringe, I was ready to feed my demons and reward myself for coming up with such a perfect plan that finally got rid of my two worst nightmares, Rah-mere and Fernando, by having their long-lost father take them out.

Loco was going to get Amanda back as I promised for doing just what I wanted, and now it was time to get mine was what I was thinking, when Velez returned without the girl.

"What the fuck are you doing? I thought I asked you to bring me the girl?" Still holding my instant feel good, I snapped.

"Oh, yeah, that, don't worry, I will, but first I'm going to help you with this," nonchalantly Velez said, raising his revolver, pumping four bullets into the still pacing the floor and mumbling to his self Darwin's back, causing me to leap to my feet and drop the syringe from my hand.

Pulling my weapon Velez's body dropped to the floor where he now laid face up, on his back, still moving and inches away from his weapon.

"You stupid motherfuck! You stupid motherfucker! Why the fuck did you do that?" Looking down at the struggling for air soon to be dead man, I shouted. "Fuck you!" Firing my .9mm I angrily said, hitting Velez between his eyes.

At the back part of the nice-size bungalow-style built home, Amanda, still handcuffed at one wrist and to a unmovable for her chair, listened to her arguing kidnappers, after hearing what she knew was guns going off, believing she would be killed next.

When I opened the door to where the frail, longhair and terrified teenager sat praying that I not hurt her, all the thoughts I was having about turning around to get the left-behind syringe and killing her no longer plagued me. "For once you're gonna do the right thing," I silently said to myself as I walked over to where Amanda, with her head down between her shivering knees held her face, not wanting to look up at me.

My beard was a snow bushy white color, looking like I hadn't shaved in weeks, as well as my eyebrows, my clothes smelled of liquor, cigarette smoke and wet dog being I'd had not taken a shower in days, to the thirteen-year-old Amanda I looked like the boogeyman she had always visioned would jump out from under her bed.

"I'm not here to hurt you. If you want to get back to your father you're going to have to trust me," I spoke from where I stood not wanting to scare Amanda any more than I could tell she was.

Her head still hanging down Amanda listened, knowing she was going to have to allow me to help her, though she did not know how to trust me.

Traveling, on our way to a Guadalajara pier where I had instructed Loco to meet and come alone, Amanda sitting quietly in the back seat, no cuffs on, and praying that everything I said to get her to believe me was true. She was missing her father, and now sat staring out the window at every car that went by looking for him.

LOCO

U sing the gate opener had gotten me closer to coming face to face with my son, Fernando, all I could do was wonder how he's going to act, not only finding me, a stranger with no right to be on his property, but when I tell him who I am.

Who do he looks like, walk like, etc. are all things I have always thought about including if him and Rah-mere resemble, or resent me at all.

Now that I have Detective Banks believing I'd went along with his request to get rid of both, Fernando and Rah-mere, to get him to release Amanda, I had to move quickly before he had learned the truth.

I have heard a lot about Fernando's vicious ways so expecting any welcome or I'm happy to see you moments coming from his way towards mine wasn't a thought, only flying bullets. The second I finished my thought, "Boom, boom, clack, clash" filled the massive mansion.

I was standing staring up at pictures hanging on the high ceiling walls, specifically at one that looked identical to me and another of Margaret looking exactly how I'd remembered her, when Fernando, creeping through the home's corridors after watching my every move from his office fired all three shots at my head using his D.E. (Desert Eagle) knocking one of his expensive pieces of art off the wall sending its glass frame shattering to the ground.

Crouching and diving, doing my best to not be victim to one of my own son's bullets, I was counting, waiting until Fernando's automatic needed reloading.

Taking eight more shots I managed to maneuver making a move behind the antique cherrywood dresser in the room.

"Come the fuck out!" Fernando angrily shouted at me, never lowing his aim still pointing his gun from where he stood behind his marble color minibar, with a better angle than he had before.

Squeezing off two more rounds missing my head by inches only made him more fiercest, and even madder seeing his expensive crystal as well as glass elevator door come crashing down. If I was gonna ever make it out of the house alive and to Amanda waiting for me to rescue her, something had to be done quick was all I was thinking as I held down my position waiting my time to strike.

Hoping my math was correct, and that I didn't miscount how many bullets Fernando had left in his clip, I stuck my head out to be greeted by two loud blasts that caused me to dash into the theatre room, and away from the hot lead, "Boom, boom, clack" Fernando's clip was finally empty.

Seeing Fernando's face for the first time brought joy and pain over my heart. He looked almost identical to Amanda. My eyes were starting to become moist, something I'd had not experienced since a kid, though I could see Fernando was trying to reload, it was time to get him to listen to what I needed him to know.

"Look, I am right here," I said walking out of the theatre room holding my weapon on my index finger upside down, exposing myself, showing that I wasn't a threat.

Staring back at what he was recognizing to be an older version of himself, Fernando strongly looked into my eyes, no longer

ready to kill and feeling his soul being taken over, he was speech-
less, though thought to his self, "How could this be?"

LOCO

After what I had just went through with getting Fernando to hear me out all I wanted to do is get Amanda back, away from Detective Banks, off the Guadalajara pier and out of Todos Santos.

I just hoped I wasn't playing another actor in another one of Banks' sinister plans.

Watching me nervously walking the pier, Detective Banks using binoculars investigated the area wanting to be sure that I came alone, from fifty yards away.

Not until he was satisfied that I did did he start out of the dark towards the pier, with a overly excited and crying early tears of joy Amanda, walking close to his side.

I was itching badly to make the devil pay for everything he had done to me and my family, something I'd dreamed every night since he'd forced me to exile, yet I knew I had to put my feelings to the side, stay focus and get Amanda out the jaws of the biggest snake I have ever seen.

"Amanda baby, everything is gonna be alright. I am going to take you home. You hear me?" I said seeing the concerned look on my little girl's face.

My rage meter spelled fury standing across from Detective Banks.

"Don't you move, Amanda."

"Okay, poppa, please, I want to go home! I'm scared!"

"I understand baby, I understand! It'll be…"

"Okay, enough of that, I'm not here for all this," the unrecognizable Detective Banks butted in.

What Banks looked like was nothing how I expected him to look and far from how I remembered him. All the years he had spent dedicating his life to destroying my family, me, Fernando, Rah-mere, and now Amanda, I could tell had worn Banks down. He looked like shit, though he still held the keys to my heart, and I knew I had to play his game.

"How do I know Rah-mere and Fernando is dead?"

"Because I gave you my word, and I am sure that your connection made you aware of it," I replied speaking of one of the undercover detectives seen with Viola at the club on the night she was murdered, when Detective Banks assisted the bullets fired from Gunem's uzi that hit her instead of him.

Kidnapping the detective, making her text Detective Banks that indeed the job was done, Rah-mere and Fernando would no longer be his problem was my first chess move towards checkmating the devil. Now I had him right where I wanted him to be, getting ready to knock the head off his king.

"You have my daughter, and you know I would never jeopardize her life. If you don't know anything about me you know that, so why don't you just take that gun out of her back and let her go. You can do whatever you want with me, just let my little girl go."

"Okay, I can do that. You stuck to your part of the deal, so I guess I can stick to mine. But first, I want you to raise up that shirt," pointing his revolver at me Detective Banks said, convinced and ready to release the still crying and pleading Amanda.

"I want to see that you're not holding. And now get down on your face," still with his weapon pointed at my face he ordered.

"Amanda baby, when he releases you I want you to run away from here as fast as you can."

"What about you daddy? What about you?" Amanda sobbed.

"I will be okay, don't you worry. I will catch up, just run and don't look back, baby," getting down to kiss the dirt as the soon to be dead man wanted me to I said and did with a aching heart.

Amanda was free running away from the pier hearing what sounded like explosions going off behind her, I was still down and ducking from gunfire feet away from where Detective Banks laid covered now in his own blood, still alive regretting he ever trusted that I had come alone.

Hiding in a deserted shack nearby the pier, Fernando taking his best shot firing one time from his Bush Master AR-15 not wanting to kill, only wound Detective Banks, when seeing him release Amanda, the little sister he couldn't wait to meet.

"Get the fuck up!" planting a kick I've waited so long to plant against the grunting in pain detective's head I shouted.

"Ahhhhh, fuck! Please, Loco, come on damn! I gave you your little girl," the bloody faced Banks pleaded to me.

"Oh, you think it's that simple, huh. Fuck you! Motherfucker! Get the fuck up, pig! You can save all that crying and begging shit for God, I am sure he don't want to hear it coming from you either," I planted another thumping sounding kick to the devil's body, this time to his ribs sending him onto his side, and out of breath.

"Get your bitch ass up and start moving," I said shoving the now grasping at his hanging shoulder and ribs Banks in the back, toward the very same road I'd pointed Amanda to run away on.

"Ahhhhh, shit! Ahhhh fuck! I can't breathe!"

"Keep moving!"

"You don't have to kill me, Loco. You don't ha..." Ending Banks' pleading thoughts I introduced his already bloody face to his own revolver.

"You forced me to leave my kids, my family, you heartless bastard! Now you're begging me for your life. You are a pathetic piece of shit! Keep fucking walking! I'm gonna show you just how smart you really are."

Reaching the waiting limousine sitting parked at the end of the road where the pier ended, I could not wait to show the battered detective how I outsmarted him. Grabbing Banks by his bushy head of hair, I wanted to be sure he saw what I had prepared solely for him.

Losing the feeling in his legs limply flopping to the ground, Detective Banks' heart stopped for a moment when seeing the using a cane to walk with one of his arms hanging in a sling Rah-mere, being helped by Fernando and Amanda step out the back of the limousine.

After I had saved Rah-mere's life killing his wife Ayah who would've killed him if I didn't stop her, as I was able to convince Fernando telling him the truth about why I had to leave his mother and him, Rah-mere agreed to go along with my plan to get Amanda back.

Rah-mere wanted nothing more than to get revenge on Detective Banks, though he'd made it clear, he wasn't going nowhere without bringing along his deceased partner's family, Angie and her two daughters, for a complete family reunion.

"Hey Banks, you look like you've seen a ghost. I guess you're not happy to see us," Rah-mere said poking at the on his knees with his face in the dirt detective, now realizing the end of his tyrant ways had finally arrived.

Detective Banks was tired and feeling like he could not handle anymore punishment. Sobbing he pleaded, wanting to live no more, yet his pleas fell on all our deaf ears.

"You don't worry, you're gonna die, just not how you think," Fernando said, speaking up for the first time while holding onto his little sister, never wanting to lose her again.

"Yeah, you are gonna die my way," I said walking over grabbing and pulling the tortured-looking Banks up from the dirt to sit on his knees.

"Come on, Loco, just put one in my head, please!"

"So that you won't feel a thing, huh, coward? After all that you've done to this family, now you want to go out the easy way?" Rah-mere questioned with noticeable rage.

"I have waited twenty-three long years for what I am about to do to your pathetic ass. I'm gonna make you pay for all the nights I lived knowing I had sons on this earth that didn't know why I wasn't there for them, for their mothers and you forcing me to leave them without a explanation, for ever getting anywhere close to my Amanda and every other gangster your greedy, slimy cracker ass has ever robbed before," I said pulling my oversize hunting knife from its holster which I wore across my chest. "This is for my family and our new connection!" I shouted into the dark island sky as loud as I could, wanting the world to hear me as I assure my family's revenge. Driving the knife straight through the devil's throat I swiftly forced the sharp blade around his thick skin neck, relieving his body of his head, finally sending Detective Banks to the hellfire where he belonged.

Detective Banks was dead and Loco finally had his family, Fernando, Rah-mere and Amanda all together for the first time like he'd always visioned, yet they all laid on their backs next to each other dying.

Jumping out of the limo's trunk, where she'd been hiding the whole time, wanting to get her own revenge, but on the family, for Fernando having been the one who ordered the hit that got her husband, Knuckles, killed and Loco's killing of her Muslim sister and best friend, Ayah, dressed wearing her all black hijab that covered her head to toe, only showing her eyes, firing a AK-47 as she was trained to as a little girl chopping Fernando, Rah-mere and Amanda down first, Angie moved in advancing like a soldier does in a war, determined to look the struggling and still fighting for his life Loco in the eyes before she kills him.

"You shot my Muslim sister in the back, you coward!" she said speaking, using her West African Guyanese accent, after spitting in his dying face.

Pressing the chopper's barrel to Loco's forehead Angie pulled the trigger four times, blowing Loco's brains all over the Todos Santos dirt ending the Connection.

Chapter 1

"That's my husband right," sitting, her and her best friend Dedria, outside on the stoop in front of Dedria's building enjoying the sixty-five-degree spring weather, the fifteen-year-old Sarah said pointing at a fresh out of prison, Pimp-Bluefish as he drove past readying to park his brand-new Cadillac.

"Who? Girl, I know you're not talking about Bluefish's old ass."

"Yup."

"Bitch! You're crazy, something is really wrong with you. Don't you know that. That man is a pimp. Don't act like you don't see all them damn prostitutes he got standing over there with their nasty-ass hands all over him. What do you think they do for him? Every last one of them bitches sell their worn out pussies for him, hoe. Do not tell me your stupid ass is over there thinking about doing no shit like that."

"Hell no, trick! You're going too far now. I'm not selling this good pussy for nobody, especially not to give my bags (money) to no man. His old ass is just cute to me, that's all. And that car needs some young bitches like us riding in it."

"No, not me, you can leave me right here."

"Bitch! Whatever, you say that now. But that thang is sexy, that color goes perfectly with my blue and white j's. I could see me now looking so damn cute, getting dropped off at school."

"Hoe, you are too damn much," Dedria laughed, shaking her head.

"I bet you one thing if I give him some of this young mee-yow he will leave all them old rags alone, I promise your hating ass that," twisting up her lips and snapping her fingers, now standing trying to get Pimp-Bluefish's attention, Sarah said.

Turning around when getting Bluefish to notice her, dig out the wedgy the booty shorts she had on caused, Sarah walked through a door she's gonna wish she never had.

"Girl, you need to sit your dehydrated ass down, that man ain't paying you any attention. Look, here comes your boo," noticing G-rock, Sarah's boyfriend, walking towards them changing the subject Dedria said receiving that look that always told her when her bestie was bothered by something. "What's up G-rock," she spoke first to the smiling ear to ear G-rock wanting to further bother Sarah, who was now giving her the stank face.

"Hey, what's up D. What's wrong with her?" G-rock asked wondering why his girl's face was all screwed up.

Leaning in to place a kiss on Sarah's cheek he was stopped getting a King James in the 2016 Finals rejection.

"Why do you have to be doing all that out here in front of everybody?" Sarah reacted, same time pushing the embarrassed G-rock at his chest and away, wanting him to stay at his distance.

"What the fuck is your problem! All of a sudden, you're out here acting like I'm doing something new. Since when I can't show you some love outside?"

Not wanting G-rock to cause a scene in front of the still-watching pimp, knowing he would follow her away, Sarah lured him out and away from the area by continuing her act, not answering.

"I am going home," Sarah said, speaking to Dedria.

"Trick, call me when you get there, and you and G-rock better not be making none of them nappy-headed babies either. I know how ya'll get when ya'll argue."

"He won't be getting none of this," smiling a broad smile while looking back and walking away, Sarah said with G-rock following in tow. Patting her shapely and still-growing ass and thighs as she spoke, she did so knowing Pimp-Bluefish had still been watching never taking his eyes off her deceptive jailbait.

From where he stood in the parking lot Pimp-Bluefish watched, his eyes locked on the young Sarah, loving the way her ass bounced and swayed side to side with her every stride.

The whole time Dedria and Sarah had been outside on the stoop, her eighty-seven-year-old Grandmother, known as Adel to everyone in the projects, stood watching looking from their third-floor apartment's window talking to her creator.

"Jesus, I know I am too old to go out there in them streets and kill that man, but I swear I wish I could. I hate him with all the heart I have left in me. So much that I wish him dead every single day. I am so sorry Lord! I know you may not let me through your heavenly gates for this. The place where I know you has placed my sweet only child's soul. I cannot and will not ever pray to you for mercy upon that evil bastard's soul. I want him dead Jesus, no longer breathing just like my Dana is. Oh Lord, I am prepared to live in the hellfire for disobeying your word to show mercy. I refuse to get down on these old weak knees to pray for him," dabbing at the wetness sliding down her no wrinkles face coming from her storied teary eyes, Adel did so meaning every word she'd prayed.

"Hey, grandma, what are you doing out of your chair?" Dedria walking into the apartment said, finding Adel still looking down and out into the projects.

"Little girl, you must think I'm old or something. Your granny still have legs, they may be weak but they do work. As long as the good Lord allows me to breathe you can betcha black tail I'm gonna crawl for what I want, if I have to young lady."

"I know that's right. Come on, let me help you back to your chair." Walking back to the window Dedria saw just who had been holding her grandmother's attention.

"Ohhhhh, grandma! I see who you had your eyes on. You got a thing for Bluefish, huh," she poked not expecting the response she got.

"Child, I want you to stay away from that man, he has three heads. You hear me! I saw how him and those nasty eyes was watching that hot in the ass friend of yours," Adel said, speaking with a sudden fire in her eyes and raspy voice that spoke loud as ever to Dedria.

"Yes grandma, I hear you." Dedria wondered why the mention of Pimp-Bluefish made Adel so angry.

"I saw how her little fast ass was out there shaking and patting on her stuff. And that filthy serpent, he was just a-watching. I swear, if I was that big yellow lady, I would hold her grown butt down, and whip the black off her back, just like my momma would've done back in the old days down south."

"You know him, momma? What, ya'll went to school together or something?"

"NO baby. Your granny knows more than you think about what goes on around here. Old Adel has lived a long life; a full eighty-seven years. I probably know that man better than he knows his self. I want you to stay far away from him, Dedria. He's no good and is on his way straight to hell on a one-way ticket."

"I hear you grandma, let me fix your pillow," Dedria said puzzled.

Dedria had no clue why Adel hated Bluefish with a passion. She could not remember no time when her grandmother showed so much hate for anybody. "My mother was killed, and I've never heard her talk ill about the person who murdered her before," Dedria thought to herself, her curiosity now getting the best of her.